HIDDEN MICKEY
ADVENTURES 1

The first novel in this Action-Adventure Mystery series about Walt Disney and Disneyland, written for all ages (9 and up).

From the author of the acclaimed HIDDEN MICKEY series.

WHAT'S MORE EXCITING THAN A DAY AT DISNEYLAND?

Ditching their family, Peter Brentwood and his younger brother stumble upon a letter from the Master Storyteller himself, Walt Disney. Following a clue in the letter they are immediately caught up in what they thought was an innocently fun treasure hunt.

SOMEONE ELSE DISCOVERS THEIR HUNT FOR HIDDEN TREASURE.

The quest takes a serious turn when someone in a trusted position begins tracking their every move, hungering for the treasure for himself.

WILL LONG-HELD SECRETS BE FORCIBLY REVEALED?

Secrets Peter's parents have closely guarded could rip their family apart if compromised. At stake is something they hold very dear: Walt's Legacy.

WATCH AS THIS YOUNGER GENERATION OF TREASURE HUNTERS GRAPPLE WITH AN IMPOSING AND FEARSOME MENACE.

Wolf, their friend and protector steps in, but is it too little, too late? Uncover secrets of Disneyland and the Disney Studios in Burbank, California, as we watch the drama unfold.

YOU WILL NEVER LOOK AT DISNEYLAND THE SAME AGAIN!

Peter and the Wolf

HIDDEN MICKEY

ADVENTURES 1

Peter and the Wolf

By

Nancy Temple Rodrigue

2012

DOUBLE-R BOOKS

HIDDEN MICKEY ADVENTURES 1
PETER and the WOLF
FIRST NOVEL IN THE HIDDEN MICKEY ADVENTURES SERIES
1ST EDITION, BOOK 1, VOLUME 2 IN THE SERIES

COPYRIGHT © 2012 NANCY RODRIGUE
LIBRARY OF CONGRESS CATALOGING-IN-PUBLICATION DATA ON FILE
www.HIDDENMICKEYBOOK.com

PAPERBACK ISBN 13: 978-0-9833975-6-4
PAPERBACK ISBN: 0-9833975-6-2
eBOOK ISBN 13: 978-0-9833975-7-1
eBOOK ISBN: 0-9833975-7-0

𝔻𝕠𝕦𝕓𝕝𝕖-ℝ 𝔹𝕠𝕠𝕜𝕤 PUBLISHED BY
RODRIGUE & SONS COMPANY
244 FIFTH AVENUE, SUITE # 1457
NEW YORK, NEW YORK, 10001
www.DOUBLE-RBOOKS.com
COVER DESIGN BY JEREMY BARTIC
 www.JEREMYBARTIC.DAPORTFOLIO.com
COVER COLOR BY CHRISNA RIBEIRO
 www.JUHANI.DEVIANTART.com
COVER COPYRIGHT © 2012 BY DOUBLE -R BOOKS
www.DOUBLE-RBOOKS.com

PRINTED IN THE UNITED STATES OF AMERICA

Dedication

*To my husband Russ
for his untiring help and encouragement
every step of the way.*

*To Kyla and Silas
for their unquenchable thirst for
fun and adventure.*

Nancy Temple Rodrigue

Disclaimer

ACKNOWLEDGEMENTS

MY SINCERE THANKS FOR ASSISTANCE IN
RESEARCH RECEIVED FROM
THE FOLLOWING MEN:

JIM KORKIS: AUTHOR OF *THE VAULT OF WALT*
JAMES KEELINE: HTTP://STRATEMEYER.ORG
MICHAEL RODRIGUEZ: ADVENTURES BY DISNEY
STEVE COOK: OFFICE OF TONY BAXTER

THANKS AND ACKNOWLEDGEMENTS ALSO GO TO
OUR PROOFREADERS AND EDITORS:
ALYSSA COLODNY
KARLA GALLAGHER, ENGLISH B.A
KIMBERLEE KEELINE, ENGLISH PH.D.
WWW.KEELINE.COM

Dear Readers,

I'd like to welcome you to *Hidden Mickey Adventures,* my new action-adventure mystery series written for the Young Adult as well as the Adult reader (age 9 and up)

In *Hidden Mickey Adventures 1: Peter and the Wolf*, you will find the same level of excitement that you have come to expect in my *Hidden Mickey* novels while encountering a few new twists and turns as the journey continues.

You will become reacquainted with some old friends from my first series of novels: *Hidden Mickey: Sometimes Dead Men Do Tell Tales!*; *Hidden Mickey 2: It All Started...*; *Hidden Mickey 3: Wolf! The Legend of Tom Sawyer's Island*; and *Hidden Mickey 4: Wolf! Happily Ever After?*   Plus, you will be making some new friends along the way.

In the opening chapter of this novel, you will find our Next Generation of clue-followers playing some of the games found in my quest book in this series: *Hidden Mickey Adventures: in Disneyland.* After hearing from so many of you that had fun solving the quest I put into the first *Hidden Mickey* novel, I saw that it was time for a book that was entirely made up of games and quests that could be enjoyed when you visit Disneyland. Walt Disney World readers also have a quest book: *Hidden Mickey Adventures: in WDW Magic Kingdom.*

So, settle back and enjoy the first adventure of Lance and Kimberly Brentwood's son Peter as he discovers his own hidden treasure from Walt Disney. And, it wouldn't be complete without assistance from our favorite security guard, Wolf!

Enjoy the adventures,
Nancy Temple Rodrigue

PROLOGUE

July 13, 1955

"It all started with a moose."

Walt Disney chuckled quietly as he stood under the flickering lanterns that lined the dock of the Mark Twain Riverboat. He was surrounded by celebrities from nearby Hollywood, local politicians, and as many friends as he could fit onto the three pristine decks waiting patiently next to the dock. In the back of the ship, the huge paddlewheel slowly churned the greenish water as if eager to begin her very first voyage.

This was a special day for Walt and Lillian. It was their thirtieth wedding anniversary and only a few days before his new Park, Disneyland, opened to the public. Special invitations had gone out to all these people surrounding Walt and he was happy and relaxed—perhaps for the first time in the year it had taken to build his dream.

His wide smile faded a little as he looked up

at the docking station. The smell of fresh paint hung in the warm summer air surrounding him. Walt's eyes narrowed as the words he had just mumbled to himself played over in his mind and remnants of a strange vision he had had about fifteen years ago came back to him. Was it a vision? A dream? He looked off into the distance, pondering. What he had seen in that strange experience had—to some extent—come true. He had seen a beautiful princess castle and a turning carrousel. He had even seen this ship.

Walt's heartbeat sped up a little. He had seen something else way back in the jungle of Columbia. This dock, this beautiful entrance to the Rivers of America had been on fire. It had been deliberately set, he recalled. *But, why?* he tried to remember. Why had someone done that to him? It had been so long ago….

His fragment of a memory faded as his wife came and took his arm. Walt's face immediately went into a warm smile as he patted her arm and led his eager guests onto the deck of the Mark Twain for the first time. It was a proud day for him.

"**W**elcome to the Golden Horseshoe, so glad that you could come," sang Slue-Foot Sue a couple of hours later, arms out in welcome as she danced across the wooden stage, the three-piece band down on the level of the audience keeping up with her lead. Servers, dressed as colorful can-can dancers, waited on the star-studded audience as the anniversary party continued.

On the second floor of the white and gold saloon, almost as high as the brilliant red velvet curtain backing the stage, sat Walt in his favorite box seat. Curved out over the stage, there were two of these railed box seats on each of the two floors. Walt preferred this box on the upper right side of the stage. Once the Park opened, he knew he would be able to sneak in up there, settle back and watch the show he enjoyed so much without being seen.

As Slue-Foot Sue was joined onstage by the Traveling Salesman, Walt leaned back on the rear legs of his spindle-legged wooden chair, happiness radiating from his face. He had done it! His Park for the whole family to enjoy together was a reality! The world would be watching in just two days when he would host Disneyland's grand opening.

His quick mind ran over steps that had led up to this moment, all the hard work, all the sacrifices. His wonderful creation of Mickey had finally put him on the map. There was the Mouse, and then there was the Moose. Walt chuckled again as he thought about the eight-minute long cartoon short he had done only five years ago titled *Morris the Midget Moose*. The moral of the story had been that two heads were better than one. Walt truly knew the value of that lesson. His brother Roy had been with him every step of this journey. Walt couldn't have done it without his brother. "It all started with a moose."

The Traveling Salesman was near the end of his routine and fired a blank-filled pistol into the air. His mind still on his musings, the sudden explosion startled Walt. His precarious perch on the back legs of the already-wobbly chair gave out and he felt himself falling backwards. Arms up to protect the back of his head, it was the rounded top of the chair that crashed into the wall just below the elaborate railing that sepa-rated the red flocked wallpaper from the white panels of the curved back wall.

Getting slowly to his feet, Walt gave an ab-sentminded wave to placate the anxious voice that asked if he was all right. He stared with dis-gust at the gaping hole he had just inadvertently created. "Great," he groused to himself. "We open in two days and I already broke some-thing!"

As his fingers traced the jagged opening that he knew could be fixed with a fresh piece of paneling in mere minutes, Walt's mind again veered toward the vision that was always some-where there, just within reach, hovering like a shadowy specter. The fire that destroyed the Mark Twain dock had been deliberate. Walt gave a sharp intake of breath as he remembered something else. Someone was trying to destroy what he had built. That was why the fire had been set. But, his mind argued, that vision, that dream, had supposedly shown things that would occur many years into the future. Yes, but it still *could* happen, couldn't it? Wasn't that the mes-sage he had been given? That everything that would happen was up to him?

"I need to protect Disneyland," Walt whis-pered out loud as the show continued below him. Always aware of what was going on around him, Walt knew the Golden Horseshoe Review was nearing the end of the performance. He was going to have to make a speech and then there would be an anniversary cake to cut with his wife, followed by dancing on the stage.

Doing what he did best, Walt came to an instant decision. "This *will be* protected," he promised himself, his eyes momentarily narrowing with determination. Righting his fallen chair, he put a smile back on his face and went to the edge of the box seat. Making a gun out of his thumb and forefinger, he "fired" back at the Traveling Salesman, bringing a laugh from the watching audience.

Yes, he would protect all that he had built. He would do everything in his power to see to it that no one could destroy what he had so carefully planned and built. With that important decision now made, he recognized that there were steps that needed to be taken and plans that needed to be made. And he knew just the man to do it.

Wolf.

CHAPTER 1

Current Day

"Hey, where is everyone?" Lance Brent-wood called as he entered his house high in the Fullerton Hills. "I risk life and limb at work every day and no one comes to greet me to see if I survived?"

"Dad, you're a security guard at Disney-land. I don't think you're going to be in a hail of bullets any time soon," Peter, the thirteen-year old, commented dryly as he came thudding down the stairs on his way into the kitchen.

With a secret smile on his face, Lance watched his son disappear down the hallway. Peter might be right on that count, but there were some things of which the boy wasn't aware regarding his dad. And his mom, too, Lance paused, thinking about it for a minute as his wife Kimberly came down the stairs in a more orderly fashion to greet her husband.

"How was your day?" the blond beauty asked as she gave him a warm hello kiss. "I don't see any new scars or injuries, so I am guessing it was good?"

Lance gave a good-natured snort as he allowed himself to be led into the kitchen. "How come no one believes I could possibly be in any danger at work?"

"Because you work at Disneyland!" came the united chorus of three male voices.

Hands on his hips, Lance looked at his three sons and slowly shook his head in disbelief. Peter had joined his brother Michael, age nine, and Andrew, age seven, as they clustered around the oak island in the middle of the huge kitchen, randomly choosing from the after-school snacks that had been laid out for them. "They're eating again. How can they *possibly* be eating again? How come they're always hungry?"

Giving him an amused laugh, Kimberly answered, "Because they are *your* sons!"

"Hmm," was all he replied as he looked over their heads at what was left of the food. There wasn't much. "You have any more of that cake?"

"That's enough," Kimberly declared, shooing all of them away from the island. "You'll all spoil your dinners."

"Aw," four male voices chimed together.

As the boys started to go their separate ways, their dad called them back. "Just a minute, guys. I saw something in the bookstore today I thought you might like."

At the word bookstore, only Michael continued to look interested. "What did you get me?

"How do you know it's just for you?" Peter challenged as he paused in the doorway just long enough to push a few of his brother's buttons.

"Because you only read under the threat of death…."

"All right," Lance stepped in. "That's enough, Peter."

"Me! He started it."

"No, I didn't!" Michael turned to his mother for back up. "Did I?"

"Hey, I just put out the snacks," Kimberly wisely stated, not wanting to get in the middle of that again. "What did you get, Lance?" she asked, her eyes telling her husband to get on with it.

Lance held up three copies of a thin blue book. "This just came out today. I thought you all would like to try it. It's called *Hidden Mickey Adventures in Disneyland* and it's a book of games and quests you can do inside the Park. It looks like fun."

At the mention of Disneyland and games, the three books were eagerly snatched out of his hands. "There's even some Junior Quests that Andrew can do, too."

Kimberly looked over Michael's shoulder as he thumbed through the book. She gave Lance a secret smile. "This looks like something we used to do at Disneyland."

He returned the look. "Kinda. Different results, I'm sure," he winked at her. "So, I thought we could try one or two of the games tomorrow."

"Tomorrow's a school day, Dad," Peter reminded him somewhat sourly.

Lance pretended to looked surprised. "It is? I thought tomorrow was Wednesday."

Andrew gave a giggle. "Dad, Wednesday *is* a school day!"

Smacking his forehead with his hand, Lance closed his eyes. "Oh, you're right. How could I forget?" He suddenly grinned and added, "I thought tomorrow was Dad Said We Didn't Have To Go To School Day."

"Lance!" Kimberly tried to break in, but was overshadowed by a loud chorus of "Yeah!"

"You all pick out which game or whatever you want to do," he called after the hoard as they rushed out of the kitchen and headed upstairs. He then turned to the narrowed green eyes of his wife. Holding up a restraining hand, he started to defend his action. "It's only one day, Kimberly. I thought we could use a fun break in the routine."

He was surprised when she didn't start to argue with him. "What I was going to say before I was so rudely interrupted," she started with a wicked glint in her eyes, "was...where is my copy?"

Lance gave her his trademark dazzling smile and immediately held up a fourth copy of the quest book with a flourish that would have impressed any magician.

"**O**kay, Andrew, watch the Dumbo elephants as they go by and find the one that's numbered twelve. What color is his hat?"

"Where are the numbers? I don't see any numbers!" The boy jumped back and forth at the black iron gate surrounding the popular ride, eagerly staring at the smiling gray elephants whizzing by overhead as they were being encouraged by Timothy the Mouse.

"See the long red arm that holds the elephants? Look way up on the arm for the number."

"I see it! I see it!" Andrew declared, getting more excited. "Nine. Ten. Eleven. Twelve! That's the one."

Off to the side, Peter was banging his game book between the posts of the fence, bored. "Mom, can Michael and I go work on the Choose Wisely multiple choice game? The quest says we have to ride Star Tours and Andrew won't go on that. Please," he remembered to throw in for good measure.

Kimberly could tell her two oldest boys were anxious to be working on their own games. "Sure, honey. Just meet us at the Golden Horseshoe for lunch at one o'clock."

"Aw, do we have to?" Michael whined. "We can just get something at the Pizza Port," he added hopefully.

Lance looked up from the souvenir map that he and Andrew were looking over to determine where to go next. "Michael Percy Brentwood."

Michael knew not to argue further. "One o'clock," he mumbled. "See you then."

With a grin on his face, Lance watched them run off in the direction of Tomorrowland. "Works every time. Just have to say their middle name and they instantly stop. Amazing."

Kimberly nodded in agreement. "I know! Surprises me every time. It used to work on me when my dad did it, too." Still smiling, she turned her attention back to her youngest son. "So, where are we going next, Andrew?"

"New Orleans Square."

She took her youngest son's hand and linked arms with Lance. "Let's go, then! You lead the way, sweetie."

"Okay," both Andrew and Lance replied at the same time. Looking at each other, they both said, "Jinx!" and laughed as they entered the wooden stakes that marked the back path into Frontierland. This quieter, shaded path behind the Big Thunder ride took them around the tall red and yellow streaked peaks of the mountain range that made them feel as if they had some-how been instantly transported to the beautiful red rock canyon country of Utah. The piercing screams coming from the riders of the train were a sharp contrast to the glassy serenity of the lake on the other side of the walkway nestled in the inviting coolness of the forest-like setting.

It was nice to get out of the warm sunshine of the brilliant spring day. The interior of the Golden Horseshoe was always cool and wel-coming. Coming in ten minutes late and ignor-ing the look their father gave them, the boys followed their family up the wide curving stair-case to the second floor. Peter was surprised when Lance led them to the box seat on the right side of stage.

"Dad, this is roped off!" he worriedly ex-claimed, lowering his voice so no one else would hear. "No one is supposed to sit here."

Lance settled them around the scarred round wooden table in the dimly-lit box. "It's okay. I got special permission."

That answer settled the boy's worry, but Kimberly gave a little laugh. She knew it simply meant Lance gave himself permission. As Lance and Peter left to get lunch downstairs, Kimberly looked out over the slowly-filling ground floor. Andrew scooted next to her to watch the crowds. Michael, though, had his nose buried in the game book, a pencil already in hand to fill in some answers. Glancing back, she could see he was working on the mixed-up words called Jumbles.

Their lunch of chicken nuggets, fries, and a wickedly delicious chocolate cake was quickly devoured and the family moved towards the edge of the box to watch the *Billy Hill and the Hillbillies* show. Michael again stayed in the back of the booth, happy to work on the puzzles.

As he referred to the souvenir map he had taken when they first came into the Park, his left foot tapped out a nervous rhythm as he gently kicked the curved back wall of the booth. Not even thinking about what his shoe might be doing to mark the wall, he filled in another an-swer. His foot kicked out again and he heard a different noise over the sound of the fiddle music coming up from the stage. It sounded like wood sliding over wood. He looked over his shoulder, but his family didn't seem to notice anything wrong. Slightly shrugging his shoulders, his foot kicked out again as his head bent back to his book. The noise happened again. Out of the corner of his eye, he saw a movement, but it was gone before he could turn his head to see what it was.

Looking back at his jumble puzzle, he was busy crossing out letters in the jumble 'contain a farce' when he heard the weird noise again. His head jerked around just in time to see an open hole in the back wall, his shoe still in contact with the wall. The sudden action he made caused his foot to jump and hit the wall at the same time. A small panel quickly slid shut, closing off the small opening.

Michael turned to get someone's attention, but thought twice about it. He wasn't sure if he would get in trouble for maybe damaging the wall or something. Instead, he put his hand on Peter's shoulder and gently shook him.

"Eat your own fries," Peter muttered over his shoulder, not even looking back to see what he wanted.

"Petey!" Michael urgently whispered, "You have to see this. Don't tell dad!"

It was the 'don't tell dad' part that got Peter's interest. Quietly scooting his chair back a little, he tried to not call any attention to himself. "What?" He could see the excitement in his brother's eyes.

"I think I found something! Or broke something," Michael added, his eyes dimming a little.

"What is it?" Peter was looking at the open

Hidden Mickey Adventures game book on the table. He didn't see why Michael would be so excited about some answer he might have figured out.

"Look at this," Michael pointed at the back wall. "I was kicking the wall," he whispered so his mom wouldn't hear him, "and this happened."

Peter watched, intrigued as Michael hit some hidden button and a small panel opened up and then slid shut again as the boy's shoe tapped it a second time.

"What do you think is in there?" whispered Michael, very pleased with himself at this discovery.

His brother could only shrug. "I have no idea. It could just be a service panel, but why would there be one so high up?"

"We need to explore this!"

"Shh!" Kimberly called over her shoulder. "Watch the show, boys."

"Yes, mom," Michael mumbled as he gave Peter one last frantic look to keep this between themselves.

Peter nodded in agreement and moved his backpack over the location where the door had slid shut again.

As soon as the funny music and joke-filled show had ended, the family gathered up their belongings and filed out of the booth. Lance placed the tasseled gold rope back in place over the red drapes that had blocked the booth and they headed outside into the bright afternoon light. The Mark Twain had just left the dock and they could hear the recorded banjo music as the white ship slowly sailed past them, her three decks filled with people.

Eager to separate themselves from their family, Peter and Michael declared they needed to go on the fast-paced Big Thunder Mountain roller coaster. Knowing they had just eaten a big lunch and, coupled with young Andrew's fear of the ride, the boys were pretty sure they would get to go alone.

They were correct. Andrew immediately shrunk back against his mother at Peter's suggestion. The seven-year old had ridden the Matterhorn Bobsleds a few times, but wasn't ready for the faster-paced runaway mine train ride just yet. And the loud screams he could clearly hear from the ride didn't help any.

Not wanting to embarrass their youngest who was torn by his own fears and still wanting to keep up with his older brothers, Lance told the two older boys to go on ahead and work on their quests. Andrew, he explained, was getting close to finishing his first game in Tomorrowland and he wanted to complete that one before they had to go home.

"Okay, buddy," Lance said to Andrew as the other two boys happily ran off towards the long line of the thrill ride, "let's go to Tomorrowland. I think there are some cars you need to identify."

Visibly relieved, Andrew clutched his new game book and led them through the fort façade that made up Frontierland's Main Street entrance. Someday he would be ready to ride Big

Thunder and then he would show his brothers he was just as brave as they were. Just not today.

From the edge of the FastPass area for Big Thunder, two pairs of green eyes watched as Lance, Kimberly and Andrew disappeared from view. Knowing Disneyland as well as they did, they knew exactly how long it would take their family to get safely out of Frontierland.

"Okay," Peter took the lead. "Let's go back to the Horseshoe. If anyone asks what we're doing up there, we can just say I am getting my backpack."

No one seemed to notice the two boys as they quickly went up the stairs. Letting the red curtain drop back into place, they crouched in the back of the booth and waited quietly for a moment. As dark as it was in the box seat and as low as they were on the floor, it was probable no one would spot them. They could see the cast members working the saloon were busy cleaning up the tables and setting up for the next show.

Talking in hushed voices, Peter asked Michael to show him exactly what he had done to open the hidden door. Always prepared, like his dad, he had dug a small flashlight out of his backpack and was holding it ready.

Michael felt all over the wall, trying to find the secret button he had hit with his shoe.

"Are you sure that's the place?" Peter suddenly asked.

Startled by the voice, Michael jerked a little causing his hand to accidently hit the right spot. Their mouths fell open as the door obediently slid open.

Peter pulled Michael back a safe distance from the wall. "Don't touch it again! We don't want it to close."

"I wasn't going to touch it again! Don't push me around like that."

Clamping his mouth shut, Peter bit back a retort on the tip of his tongue. He knew Michael was excited and a little scared. "Sorry," he muttered. "Here's my flashlight. See if you can see anything."

Michael took the peace offering and smiled as he aimed the light into the darkness. "I don't see anything but wood and dust. It doesn't look like anything is in here."

Peter could hear the disappointment in his brother's voice. "Do you want me to look?" he offered.

Nodding, Michael reluctantly scooted back and handed Peter the light. As Peter's head and hand disappeared into the hole, Michael glanced over his shoulder. He froze when he saw a couple of cast members straight across from them cleaning out the other upper box.

Peter, unknowing of any of this, gave a muffled, "I think I see something," just as Michael whispered for him to turn off the light. "What?"

"Don't move." Michael froze, his back pressed up against the wall and his eyes glued on the two women talking together while they worked. He waited breathlessly until they finished wiping off the table and left the booth. "They're gone," he tapped Peter's shoulder.

Oblivious to what had just happened, Peter pulled his head out. "Who's gone?"

"The two ladies cleaning the box across from us...over there," Michael pointed, breathing hard. "I thought they were going to see us."

Alert now, crouched down low, Peter edged to the side of the box and peered through the white spindles. He could see the two women were slowly working their way through the tables and chairs on the second floor. "I think we need a diversion. I found something nailed to one of the beams, but I need a little time to get it. Do you think you could do something to make everyone look at you?"

Michael, never wanting to be the center of attention, cringed a little. "Do I have to? Why can't I get whatever you found and you make the noise?"

"I don't think you can reach it. My arms are longer," Peter told him, understanding his brother's hesitation. "Here's my thought. Just like we do at home when Mom's not around, you slide down the banister of the stairs. Hoot and holler like we usually do."

At the skeptical, worried look on Michael's face, Peter added, "Listen, it's the only thing I can think of. The worst thing they can do is throw us out of the building and tell us not to do that again."

"You sure?"

"Uh, yeah," Peter quickly replied, hoping he was right. He realized that he and Michael were

pretty well known throughout the whole Disneyland resort since both his mom and dad worked
there. It was possible the cast members could
somehow page his dad to come and get them.
Then he and Michael would have to explain what
they were doing back inside the Horseshoe.
"Yeah, it should work just fine," he said confi-
dently—more for himself than Michael. "Give
me a minute to pull the gray thing loose and then
let her rip. Go ahead now, and make it loud."

Michael's face was not the vision of confi-
dence as he headed for the top of the stairs.
The banister didn't frighten him. It was a wide
brass one that gently curved down to the bottom
floor. The banister at home was much longer
and steeper. It was the possibility of getting
caught and getting in trouble and being embarrassed that worried Michael. He gave a sigh as
he watched his Mickey Mouse watch tick
through the seconds.

Back in the private booth, Peter smiled
when he heard a loud, "Yahoo!" as Michael took
off down the banister, whooping it up as he went.
With a firm yank, Peter finally freed the flat canister that had been tacked to an upper beam.
Stuffing it in his backpack, he finally found the
button to close the secret panel and hurried out
of the booth. Running down the stairs, he could
see that his red-faced brother was surrounded
by angry, concerned cast members.

"Michael, you could have really hurt yourself," a pretty server named Dawn was telling
him. "You should know better!" She looked over
as Peter loudly thumped down the last couple of

steps as he tried to draw some the focus and attention away from his brother. His plan had only partial success. "And Peter." Her eyes were smiling even though she maintained a severe frown on her face. "I would have expected that trick out of you, not Michael. Is your dad here?"

The boys looked at each other. "Uh, he's with mom and Andrew doing a game. We were just on our way over there," he waved vaguely towards Tomorrowland, "when I saw I left my backpack here during the show." He held it up for everyone to see. "We're sorry," he smiled. "Michael won't do it again. Will you, Mikey?" he asked, punching him on the shoulder.

Frowning at the sudden assault on his arm, he glared at his brother. At the insistent look on Peter's face, Michael's mouth formed a silent, "Oh." Taking Peter's hint, he broke into a wide smile and gazed up at Dawn. "Uh, no, I won't," he promised as sincerely as he could fake.

Dawn looked at both of the handsome faces smiling up at her. It wasn't hard to see who their dad was—and that he had trained them well. She had difficulty keeping the severe look on her face. "All right, I'll let you off this one time. But, no more foolishness like that. Am I understood?"

"Yes, ma'am," they both mumbled trying very hard to look sorry.

Dawn just slowly shook her head back and forth as the boys hurried out of the saloon. "Just like their dad," she muttered to the other cast members who were standing there watching the goings-on.

More than one head nodded in agreement

as they all got back to work.

CHAPTER 2

"We did it!" Michael breathlessly proclaimed as they ran into Magnolia Park next to the Haunted Mansion in New Orleans Square. They wanted to put some distance between themselves and the Golden Horseshoe—plus go in the opposite direction of where they thought the rest of their family might be.

"That was so cool! I can't believe you really slid down the banister!"

Michael was still excited and couldn't stand still. Weaving back and forth, he looked like he wanted to break out and run somewhere. "I know! I was going pretty fast by the time I got to the bottom! What did you find? What did we get?"

They found a quiet spot in the shade near the exit of the stream train. People were coming and going from the Haunted Mansion FastPass center, but no one really paid any attention to the two boys. Peter still took a moment to look around before he pulled off his backpack.

"I think we're okay here," he finally said when the last of the disembarking passengers from the steam train had filed by. Reaching into his pack, he retrieved a flat, gray plastic container. It was about twelve inches long and ten inches wide but only about three inches thick. Peter pulled out the two short nails that had secured it to the beam and set them aside. Then, lifting the case to his ear, with Michael scarcely breathing at his every movement, he gently shook the case and heard a dull thump inside.

"What is it? Do you hear anything?"

"What?" In the excitement, Peter had actually forgotten his brother was sitting next to him, anxiously awaiting any news. "Oh, there is something inside. It isn't exactly rattling around, but there is something."

"How do we get it open?" First reaching out for the capsule, Michael pulled his hands back to his sides, and then reached out again. He would have grabbed it if he had any idea on how to get it open, but finally decided to let his older brother go ahead.

Mindless of his brother's actions, Peter was examining the gray container closely. "It looks like this end opens. I'll see if I can just pull it out."

Peter was quickly learning that this hidden treasure didn't want to come easily. He couldn't seem to find an easy grip and his fingers kept slipping down the smooth surface. "I need something to pry it open. I don't suppose you have a screwdriver on you, do you?"

"Why would I have a screwdriver at Disneyland? Use your teeth," was Michael's less-than-helpful suggestion.

"I'm *not* going to use my teeth. Wait a minute, I might have something," as Peter dug into the dark depths of his backpack. He pulled out various items and dismissed them one by one. Pens, stylus, a First Visit button he asked for at City Hall, gum wrappers, a length of twine, unfinished homework he quickly stuffed back inside before Michael could see it and tell Mom, a stubby pencil with the eraser chewed off, a couple of rocks, a CD, his phone. "Ah, here it is."

"What are you doing with a can opener?"

"I don't know," he honestly told Michael, staring at it in wonder as he held it up in front of them. "I saw an extra one in the kitchen and guess I forgot put it back." He shrugged it off and carefully tried to wedge the thinner end of the can opener between the tight end cap and the base of the container. His patience was rewarded as the plastic moved a fraction of an inch and he was able to slide the metal opener further into the new opening. As the end cap of the container began to finally pull out, both boys found they were holding their breath, excitement shining in their green eyes.

The end cap finally came off with a soft *Pop*. Peter looked over at Michael, who was holding his lower lip between his teeth, and asked him, "Do you want to find out what's inside? After all, you found the secret opening, not me."

A look of pleased gratitude crossed over Michael's face. Still, he said, "No, no. You do it. You're the oldest."

"What does that have to do with anything?"

"Just do it," Michael urged him, not wanting to admit he was still a little scared that they might have done something wrong. "You look."

Never one to back down from any adventure, Peter silently shrugged his willingness. "Okay, here goes."

He tilted the capsule toward him and a bunch of yellow-edged papers tumbled out, one of them weighted down with something. Within the folds of the papers they could see something clear peeking out. After another quick glance around to see if anyone was too close to them, Peter held up the heaviest piece. "Pennies?" He sounded as if he couldn't believe it. "Someone went to all that work to hide pennies?"

"Hey! They look like a Hidden Mickey!" Michael pointed out, sitting so close to Peter that he was almost in his brother's lap.

Peter took another look and gave a laugh. The pennies were actually glued to the paper so they all touched and were set in a very familiar shape. "You're right! Bet you won't find that one in the maps. There's a lot of writing on the other pages, like it's a letter or something."

"What's on that clear thing?"

Peter carefully pulled out the thick, clear film. They both gasped. "It's a hand-painted cel of Mickey. It looks really different compared to what he looks like now. Oh…," he broke off, his hands starting to shake a little.

"What is it? What's wrong?" Michael got instantly worried at the sudden change in his brother's look.

Peter's mouth opened to answer him, and

then closed again. He just pointed to the lower corner of the animation cel and handed it to Michael.

Michael didn't want to touch it until he knew what was wrong. He peered closer to read what was written there. "Walt Disney. It says Walt Disney."

Peter's slightly pale face turned to face him. "Michael, it doesn't just *say* Walt Disney. That *is* Mr. Disney's signature. He must have personally drawn this Hidden Mickey."

"How do you know that?"

"Dad and Uncle Adam were talking one night about Walt's signature. They both said how hard it was to find real signatures from Walt, how valuable they were. Uncle Adam has one that Aunt Beth proved was a fake. He said he had paid a lot of money for it…." Peter realized he was rambling in his excitement. He took a deep breath before he finished. "Anyway, I asked them to show me what a real signature would look like…. And guess what? It looked exactly like this!"

The importance of this find began to sink in with Michael. "Wow," he whispered. "That's really cool." Getting nervous again, he suddenly pushed Peter's hand that was holding the cel away from him. "Put it away! Put it away out of sight, Petey. Don't let anyone else see it. They might take it away from us." He looked anxiously to the left and the right as if assassins were about to close in on them. When he seemed satisfied that they were at least momentarily safe, his eyes still wide, Michael whispered,

"What does the other stuff say?"

Agreeing with Michael's desire for secrecy at this point, Peter carefully covered the animation cel between the blank papers that had originally protected it and slid them back into the capsule. Not immune to the importance and excitement of the find, he took a moment to steady himself before he lifted up the letter. In a hushed voice he started reading; so hushed that Michael had to lean in a lot closer to hear him.

"Hello, there. I'm your host, Walt Disney.

"Sounds kinda formal, doesn't it? That's the way a lot of my television shows are introduced. Since this little Park of mine is an extension of those shows, I thought it was fitting to greet you that way.

"If you are reading this, you must have found my hiding place. The Golden Horseshoe, as well as the rest of my Park, is very special to me. I don't know when you will find this note of mine, but I hope you are still enjoying the show.

"It came—somewhat vividly—to my attention that all I have created needs to be protected. I have more than one system in place and some key people already at work. But, time happens to all people. Time continues and people change, move on, or even die.

"I want my Park to keep going long after I am gone and I hope you can help me with that task. If it sounds too much for you, go no further, keep the trinket I have enclosed, and put the capsule and this letter back where you found them. Someone else will surely come along someday.

"But, if you are willing, keep going and see where this Hidden Mickey adventure will take you. I hope it will be a fun quest.

"Your first clue is centered on someone I really admire: Charlie Chaplin.

"Best wishes, Walt."

Peter quit reading and stared at the pages. When he remained silent, a confused Michael looked up at him and asked, "What does he mean? He said 'your first clue' and then he just said 'Charlie Chaplin.' I...I don't get it. What kind of a clue is that?"

Peter turned the note over, but there was nothing written on the back. "I don't get it either. What else is there? Check the penny page."

"Here it is!" Michael almost yelled as he flipped over the page that had the pennies glued to it. He thrust it at Peter. "You read it. I can't make out the curly letters very well."

"Take this with you and go see the boy who never grew up. He will tell you where to go next. Remember, if at first you don't succeed, try, try, try, try again. Bring some pennies!"

"The boy that never grew up.... He has to mean Peter Pan.... But, how do we get Peter Pan to tell us where to go?" Peter scratched his sandy blond hair.

"How do you know he means Peter Pan?" Michael challenged, frowning as he stared hard at the old paper as if willing it to divulge its secrets.

Peter looked off towards Fantasyland, a contemplative frown between his own eyes. "It has to mean Peter Pan. Who else would be the boy who never grew up?"

"You mean, besides you?" Michael suddenly grinned and swerved away enough so Peter's gentle swing missed his arm. "Okay, so *I* think we need to read the story."

"Or ride the ride," Peter shrugged again as he weighed their options. "We are here in Disneyland." He briefly thought that it might be a good idea to ask his dad about this, not knowing that his dad had also experienced one of Walt Disney's quests a few years back. But he *really* wanted to see if he could figure this out by himself.

In the excitement of their discovery of the letter and a hidden clue—and the possibility of more treasure that they were subconsciously building up in their minds—both of the boys had completely overlooked what the letter had told them. The letter seemed to imply that there would be some form of responsibility that they would be assuming by continuing to follow what Walt had put into place so long ago.

1956

"**S**ay Walt," one of his animators stopped him in the hallway, "did you hear what happened on the Peter Pan Ride yesterday?"

Head down, Walt had been on his way to a storyboard meeting. At the mention of one of his favorite attractions, he stopped in his tracks and gave the man his full attention. "No, what happened? Anything I need to take care of?"

"No, no," the man chuckled, waving off his concern. "Well, I guess it could have been bad, under the circumstances," he broke off, looking off into the distance, his hand on his chin.

Not liking the sound of that, Walt's eyes narrowed. "Maybe you need to tell me the whole story," as he folded his arms over his chest and waited.

Knowing he needed to do this quickly, the animator dove right in. "Well, first off, no one was hurt, okay?" Seeing a look of alarm come into his boss's eyes, he added, "No, really, they are fine. See? This older couple was riding Peter Pan and the ride broke down. They were right at the part where Mr. Smee is pointing his gun at the boats flying overhead and Captain Hook is shouting for him to 'shoot them down!' Well, right then, the mechanism holding the pirate ship broke and they came falling out of the sky! They walked out of the ride and were rubbing their hips. The gals working the ride, of course, rushed right over to them and asked if they were all right, if they needed a nurse. This couple laughed it off and said, 'We love this ride! Can we go ride it again?' When told the ride was broken, they just walked off smiling and said they would be back later."

Walt, once he knew the couple involved was really all right, was relieved and could smile at the humor of the incident. He knew things could happen with mechanics. Rides broke down all the time. It just was hopeful that guests wouldn't be there when it did happen and possibly get hurt. His mind, always quick, jumped to a related story. Leaning against the wall of the corridor in which they were standing, Walt got a far-away look in his eyes. "Did I ever tell you my story with Peter Pan?"

The animator thought he had heard the story once before, but never minded listening to the boss relate some fascinating bit about his past. "Come on in my office and have a chair, Walt. I'd like to hear it."

Once they were seated, the storyboard meeting pushed to the side of his mind, Walt leaned back in his chair. Warming up to the subject, he rubbed his hands together as he transported both of them back almost forty-five years in time to Marceline, Missouri, where Walt had spent some of the happiest days of his life. "There was a traveling show that was doing *Peter Pan*, gosh, I don't know, sometime around 1909 or 1910. It was Maude Adams who played the lead. There were all kinds of posters plastered all over town. You can just imagine how exciting it was to an eight or nine-year old boy like myself," Walt was saying, leaning forward now, his elbows on his knees. "Why, I had to break into my piggy bank to afford to go, but, by golly, Roy and I bought tickets! I'll never forget those two hours that took us into Never Land. Did you know I got to play Peter Pan in a school play?" he asked, not really stopping to wait for an answer. "No actor ever identified himself with the part he was playing more than I. And I got to do something I had always wanted to do. I got to fly!" Chuckling now, he slowly shook his head back and forth as that day came vividly back to mind. "It was at my elementary school there in Marceline. Roy used some kind of block and tackle rigging to get me up into the air. It worked pretty good, too…right up to the moment it broke! You should have seen the looks on the faces in the audience as I flew right into them!"

Chuckling along with his boss, the animator then asked, "Is that one of the reasons you worked so hard at getting the rights to the book?"

Walt's head snapped back at the question. He had actually forgotten where he was, lost as he was in his special memory. "Rights? Oh, yeah. It took two years of negotiations before we got the rights. I wanted to work on *Peter Pan* right after *Bambi* was released, you probably remember. But, there was so much I wanted to do with the story that couldn't be done properly just then. We all knew animation was constantly improving, so I just had to be patient."

Nodding, the animator added, "Yeah, another eleven years before it came out. That's a lot of patient!"

Walt got to his feet, knowing he had to get to the storyboard meeting. "But, it was worth the wait! Let me know if there any more mishaps at the Park, all right?"

"You got it, boss."

Disneyland – Current Day

Peter added the pages of the letter to the animation cel inside the gray capsule and returned it to his pack. He kept out the penny page as the note had said to bring that along. "Let's go ride Peter Pan and see what happens. Maybe the pennies will set off a hidden sensor and we'll win a prize."

Standing in line for the popular dark ride that flies the guests in their own pirate ship over the rooftops of London and around the colorful peaks of Never Land, the brothers didn't have much to say to each other. Both of them were thinking of possible cool prizes they might get. When it was their turn to ride, they eagerly leaned forward against the black padded restraining bar as their red and white-sailed ship lifted up off the ground and swung around the Darling's nursery. Craning their heads, they looked at every possible thing in the rooms. But, by the time their ship dropped down into the battle scene between Peter and Captain Hook, the boys were a little deflated.

"I don't see anything different. Do you, Peter?"

"No, it is just the same as it always is. Nothing got set off by the pennies. Maybe we did it wrong. We're at the mermaids already. Let's ride it again."

Michael stifled a groan. This wasn't one of

his favorite rides. He liked Mr. Toad's Wild Ride better. "'Kay."

The next time through, Peter and Michael switched places in the pirate ship. "Anything, Peter?"

"No. Let me see that paper."

"You can't read in the dark."

"Just give it to me, Michael!"

"Hey, why is it glowing?"

"I don't know. What did you do to it?"

"I didn't do anything to it! What did you do to it, Peter?"

A little frantic, Peter turned the oddly-glowing sheet in question over. On the back of the page, they could clearly see it was yellow letters that were glowing. "It's a hidden message!" he gasped excitedly.

Their pirate ship turned a corner and the black light effect faded so that they could no longer see the hidden words. Impatiently, the boys stared at the paper until they entered the next room filled with special effects. They could see the words 'Chaplin Mutoscope' which made no sense to either of them. The message faded again as they entered the mermaid scene and their pirate ship came to a stop at the unloading platform.

"It has to be the lighting in the ride that set off the letters," Peter was explaining as they pushed out of the black iron exit gate and let it bang shut behind them. "Like the handstamp you get when you leave the Park. Remember? We need to find a black light and see the words again. I only recognized the word Chaplin."

"Don't all the rides in here use that same lighting?" Michael asked, hoping they weren't going to have to ride Peter Pan again.

"Yes, but most of the rides are so short I don't know if we would have time to figure out the other word."

Michael glanced at his watch and then held it helpfully out for Peter to see. "We're supposed to meet Mom and Dad in less than an hour and go home."

Giving a groan as a reply, Peter had forgotten all about his family in all this excitement. He made a quick decision. "Let's try riding Alice in Wonderland. I think it has the most black lights. Remember how funny your white shirt always looked all the way through the ride? I'll read off the letters and you write them down. You still have your pen and the game book, right? Use that. Then we'll meet Mom and Dad and figure this out at home. Okay?"

"Just you and me?" Michael asked kind of shyly. He liked the idea of working alone on something new and fun like this with his older brother.

Peter looked at the hopeful face of Michael. Usually their family did things together as a unit, but he thought he understood that it was Michael's desire to keep this just between the two of them. "Yeah," Peter lightly punched him in the arm, giving him a big smile. "Just you and me."

As they walked towards the edge of Fantasyland and the Alice ride, Peter thought of something else. "Hey, Michael, remember the last time we went over to Uncle Adam and Aunt Beth's house? Right after the twins broke that vase?"

"Yeah," Michael snorted. "I thought Alex and Catie were really going to get in trouble for that! You know, I really like their dog Sunnee. You think Dad will let us get a dog now?"

"I don't know," Peter said impatiently, not wanting to be sidetracked by a discussion about a possible pet. "Listen, remember over their fireplace? Uncle Adam was showing us all those Snow White animation cels he had put into frames and hung up there."

"What about them?" as they wound through the shady chain-linked queue. Michael was still thinking about their friend's huge Golden Retriever, Sunnee.

"They were the same size as...," Peter clamped his mouth shut as his eyes darted around. No one seemed to be listening to him. Lowering his voice to a whisper anyway, he continued, "They were just the same size as the Mickey we found. And they were also signed. Isn't that weird?"

"I don't know. Should we ask Mom about the dog? Andrew is already seven and our house is bigger than Uncle Adam's. Do you think Aunt Beth would let me drive her keel boat now? I am nine. Alex got to drive it and he's only eleven."

Used to Michael's sudden thought shifts and random questions, Peter didn't answer his brother. He was thinking about animation cels and Walt Disney.

As the boys went to meet the rest of their family with the new clue safely stowed in Peter's backpack, a red warning light was blinking on and off on a map in a secret room in the nearby city of Fullerton, high in the hills. This locked, unmarked room located on an upper floor was called the War Room and there were only three people alive on the earth who knew about it.

The map was a large holographic map of Disneyland that glowed and shimmered and hung in the air in the middle of the huge room. There were also a bank of computers and information stations, a large filing cabinet system, monitors that showed live feed from countless hidden cameras throughout the Park, and a wall of telephones in that room. With the touch of a button on the main console, the map of Disneyland could be instantly replaced with a map of the world—also showing many yellow dots here and there around the globe.

This room had been designed and built by Walt Disney himself decades earlier. The building in which the room was hidden was also designed by Walt and presented as a gift to the man who would watch over and protect all that Walt had built—his first Guardian. When that man had suddenly died several years ago, his daughter and son-in-law had proven themselves to be worthy of taking over the role as Guardians of Walt.

The blinking red dot of light was surrounded by many solid yellow dots. Each of those lights indicated special places to Walt that he wanted protected—no matter what was going on in Disneyland. They could pinpoint rides that he didn't want changed, or they could indicate something special that he wanted to remain in place—like the petrified tree he had given to his wife as an anniversary present and soon thereafter found a place in Frontierland to remain forever. Or, more importantly, they could represent hidden clues or messages Walt had put into place to preserve his legacy. When a light turned red and started blinking, it meant that something Walt had put there had been found, removed, or damaged. It was then up to the Guardians to find out what had happened and either fix it or observe what was going on and act accordingly.

The red light that just started to go on and off was located on the west side of Disneyland, in Frontierland. It indicated that something happened inside the Golden Horseshoe. Only, there was no one in the War Room to see the warning light. The Guardians were not at their post.

For the War Room was located on the third floor in the mansion where the Brentwood family lived and two of the three Guardians—Kimberly and Lance—were having a fun day at Disneyland with their boys Peter, Michael, and Andrew.

Chapter 3

"It takes a thief to catch a thief," Theodore Raven smiled to himself as he patrolled the shops of Main Street U.S.A. It was a bright, warm Saturday, one of the busiest days in Disneyland. Dressed in casual clothes consisting of khaki shorts and a Hawaiian shirt, he wandered in and out of the stores looking for possible pickpockets or shoplifters.

Theodore, or Todd to most people, despite all his efforts to be known as Raven, preferred working the Fox Patrol over his usual assignment of late-night security guard. This Fox Patrol was an undercover position in Disneyland's Security Department designed to quietly apprehend thieves working within the Park. He had been trained by the best of the Force, Wolf. His admiration of Wolf and his abilities led Todd to try and change his own moniker to Raven, thinking that title would make him sound edgier and more dangerous. But, to no avail. His nametag, now hidden from view under the loud Hawaiian shirt, still proclaimed him to be Todd.

Following one likely suspect from the Emporium across Main Street into the Disney Clothiers shop, Todd kept an eye out for other likely marks for his own use. There was one thing Wolf never learned in Todd's background check when he was hired at Disneyland two years ago: Todd himself was an accomplished liar as well as a seasoned thief. And what better place to work his trade than in a popular amusement Park filled with tourists and all their tourist dollars, traveler's checks, and credit cards?

Todd had been doing very well since he was hired—both as a security guard for Disneyland and at his secret profession as a pickpocket. He had a brilliant record of apprehensions of thieves. What the record failed to show, though, was that approximately half of all the money or goods that were recovered were never reported as missing or stolen. He knew that the average tourist had no idea exactly how much cash had been in the wallet that had been stolen from their purse or back pocket, or just how many credit cards had been stuffed inside. Todd saw that he could start making a lot of easy money on the sly, and that's exactly what he did. To keep suspicion at a minimum he only gave half the money he recovered from his supposedly 'lost' wallets to the unknowing Disneyland office, and he stole quite a few wallets to keep for himself.

Like most thieves, Todd was very smug and thought quite highly of his own abilities. Pulling one over on the intrepid, well-respected Wolf was quite a big deal in his mind. Chuckling to himself, Todd felt it was a shame he couldn't share the knowledge of his abilities with anyone else. Keeping to himself within the Security Force, he was mostly known to be a loner—another wasted effort to heighten his perceived image and earn the nickname Raven.

As Todd followed a sticky-fingered guest into the Crystal Arts, his interest wavered. Other than a couple of Goofy pens the man had stuck into his pocket back in the Emporium, he didn't seem to be able to find anything easy to pick. Todd knew that the colorful pens weren't worth the time it would take to process the man and throw him out of the Park. Alerting the woman cast member working the cash register that there was a possible thief in the store, he left her to watch the man as he returned to Main Street. Regulations required that he would be called if the man decided to go for a bigger haul.

Standing on the sidewalk, Todd let the ebb and flow of the guests move around him. People were coming and going at various speeds depending on whether they were just coming into Disneyland to begin their day of adventure and fun, or whether they were dragging sullen children out of the Park to go to lunch somewhere else or, worse, to go home. Seeing a woman with a small child and a baby stroller— along with an open purse—struggling when the wheels of the stroller as they got stuck in the horse trolley tracks, he rushed over to help. As he helped lift the stroller out of the tracks, he also helped himself to her wallet by lifting it out of the

gaping purse. Grateful for the help, the unknow-
ing victim smiled her thanks and continued up
Main Street towards Sleeping Beauty Castle and
Fantasyland.

With the wallet safely hidden in the deep
pocket of his cargo shorts, Todd looked around
for whatever else he could find. He preferred
working the Emporium right near the time the
Park was closing. People were most frantic to
make last-minute purchases and were quite un-
mindful of how they carried their purses and wallets. Now, however, it was just after noon. The
guests were more interested in lunch and finding
a nice quiet location in some shade.

As he was walking down Main Street to
head over to the Hungry Bear Restaurant and
its tightly-packed, inattentive guests, he couldn't
help but notice two boys in the Penny Arcade.
Kids usually spent a little time in the arcade, trying out the different old-time games and machines. However, since they were used to the
modern, high-tech video games, most kids
quickly tired of the old machines you had to
crank by hand or games that had limited targets.
As he neared the brightly-lit entrance, he paused
next to Esmeralda, the fortune teller's box. Not
interested in having his fortune revealed for a
quarter, he peered more closely at the boys.
They had looked somewhat familiar to him. But,
what was more interesting to Todd was that they
seemed to be awfully interested in one particular machine, not having left it since he spotted
them.

Their heads had been bent close together,

as if sharing great secrets that only the two of them could know. When they broke apart to look at the machine in front of them, Todd recognized them as one of his fellow security guard's kids. These two had to be Lance Brentwood's boys. He had seen the whole family together at different Park events—especially noticing what a beauty Lance had married. He couldn't remember the boys' names just then, but he wondered why they were acting so funny. Referring to a beat-up piece of paper again and again, they kept comparing it to the old-fashioned movie projector in front of them. Todd could see by the title card on the top of that particular machine that it starred Charlie Chaplin in something called "Dough and Dynamite."

Slowly he moved closer, fishing in his pockets to find some coins to operate the bright green and gold machine that was located next to theirs. Spaced about four feet apart, he figured he wouldn't alert them to his interest. As he turned the crank, he barely watched the cards flipping over to show him the "Battling Twins." He now could clearly hear the younger, shorter boy talking.

"Are you sure this is the right one, Peter?"

Peter again referred to his notes. "Well, I showed you what I found on the Internet last night on Mutoscopes. They were invented back in 1894 and they have about 850 different cards like a cartoon flipbook. When you turn this crank," he pointed to the recently painted machine, "the pictures fall past this viewer one at a time, but the flip action makes it look like a real moving picture. It only lasts about a minute. The reference said they were used in penny arcades a long time ago. That's how I figured it might be here."

Now assuming the boys were just doing some sort of research, maybe for a school project on old picture machines like this, Todd was just about to turn and walk away when he saw the younger boy look around the Penny Arcade, a frown on his face. The boy didn't notice when he hurriedly ducked back down to look in his own Mutoscope. "I guess," he was saying. "It looks like this is the only one that has Charlie Chaplin in it. What do we do now? Did you bring the pennies Walt left us?"

Todd's interest piqued again when Peter seemed to shush the younger boy's reference to a Walt. It could be anyone named Walt, but why the secrecy?

"Shh, don't say that too loud, Michael. No, I brought some out of Andrew's piggy bank. Hey, don't give me that look! I left him a shiny quarter instead."

Peter now referred to a different piece of paper in his hand. "It says to try, try, try again if we don't succeed. I'm not sure what we are supposed to see. Do you want to do it first?" he asked, holding out a penny.

"Me?" Michael looked shocked. "No! You do it," as he pushed the coin back at Peter.

Peter stifled a groan at his brother's reluctance. "Tell you what, let's both look. If I take the right side of the viewer, you can have the left side. Put your right eye on the view thing. We can both watch while I turn the crank to make the pictures move. How does that sound?"

Michael moved to the left side of the colorful machine. It was almost too tall for him as it was designed for adults to watch the show. Standing on his tip-toes, he said, "Okay, I'm ready."

"Here goes." Peter dropped in a penny and started turning the crank. The darkness inside the view screen suddenly lit and they could see faded images of Charlie Chaplin dressed as a baker. There was another man who seemed to be in competition with Charlie. They tried to sabotage each other's work and a stick of dynamite was put into a loaf of bread. The oven finally exploded as the images faded from view and the screen faded back to black.

"That's it? I don't get it," Michael moved aside a little to look at Peter. He had been pressing his face so hard against the machine that it left curved marks on his forehead. Giving a sudden smile, he added, "I did like the dynamite part!"

"You would," his brother retorted with a smug grin, deciding not to mention the dents on Michael's face. "The note said to try, try again, so let's do another penny."

Their two heads huddled close together again as the motions were repeated—with the same results. Peter dropped in a third penny and tried to turn the crank faster this time. However, the images moved at the same rate of speed and they saw the same movie a third time.

"Again?" asked Michael eagerly. He really liked the oven exploding and flour going all over the two men.

A fourth penny was dropped in and Peter turned the bright crank. But, after the third rotation, the screen went suddenly blank and they could hear the sound of something automated moving inside. Afraid to take their eyes off the viewer, the boys held their breath as the noise quickly stopped and the screen lit up again.

As Todd continued to listen in to what was being said, he too heard the strange noise coming from a machine known for its quietness. Since the boys were glued to the eyepiece, he stopped pretending to watch his own show. This was proving to be much more interesting than he had hoped.

Peter, totally immersed in what he was doing, continued to crank and the screen came back into focus in the Mutoscope. However, the image had changed from Charlie Chaplin to that of someone very familiar.

"It's Walt!" Peter whispered needlessly to his brother.

"Keep turning," whispered back Michael, kicking out with his foot.

"I am turning. Just watch."

The black and white images—much clearer than the images of Chaplin—showed the camera pulling back from a close-up of Walt's smiling face. It revealed him to be in a tropical setting. He was holding a long stick in his right hand and he walked over to a parrot above his head and tapped the perch on which the bird was sitting. His lips moved, but there was no sound. A black card edged in curly white lines popped into view and read: "Wake up, Jose!" As the parrot started moving and the perch turned this way and that, Walt put his fingers to his lips and motioned for the camera—and the viewer— to follow him. He walked over to the right to a wall in the room and pointed at a totem pole of faces. He pointed at the topmost face with his stick, tapped it twice, and the light faded a little with Walt frozen in position.

Peter found the crank no longer turned as the previous noise sounded inside the machine again. As the boys stared, afraid to move, the new cards that had appeared with Walt on them began to turn dark and fall off the circular reel that held them. It was as if they were turning to dust right before their eyes. When the last of the new cards looked like they were completely destroyed, the Mutoscope whirred again and Charlie Chaplin came back into view, his little movie continuing. When it finished, the viewscreen went completely dark again.

As fast as he could, Peter inserted another coin and another, trying it again and again. But, no matter how many times he did it, he was only shown the 1914 film "Dough and Dynamite."

"We broke it," Michael whispered, his face white.

They both backed away from the Mutoscope. Peter didn't quite agree. "No, I don't think so, Mikey. I…I think that was what we were supposed to see. I hope."

"You…you don't look too sure," Michael

said, his chest rising and falling with rapid breathing.

"Come over here, away from the machine," Peter pulled on his brother's arm, his eyes wide with indecision.

As soon as they walked a ways off, a man in a very colorful shirt immediately took their place at the Mutoscope and inserted his own penny. The boys warily watched him for the time it took the film to play, and then the man inserted another coin. They could tell by his actions that he saw the same Chaplin movie again when he lost interest and wandered over to a rifle game located next to them and put in a quarter to play.

Ignoring him once again, the boys returned to their previous discussion. Todd had to really strain to hear them as his rifle popped ineffectively at the unmoving targets.

"I think I know where we are supposed to go next. I saw Walt do that same thing in a special edition movie we watched. Remember?" Peter asked, staring at his brother, willing him to know what he was talking about. "They had bonus features that Mom and Dad love to watch. Walt was in the Tiki Room. They still do it today to start the show. Sometimes they let a kid from the audience wake up Jose, the lead parrot."

"Yeah, I know that part, Peter. I'm not stupid." Michael was still nervous that they may have broken the ancient movie machine and would get in trouble for it.

"I didn't say you were stupid! Gosh, where did that come from?"

Michael just looked miserable. "We'll have

to wait until after the show to look in that mouth. You know for sure which one it is? What if we get caught?"

"We can always say we are looking for our dad."

"Oh, if we get caught, I'm sure he'll find us," Michael groaned.

Peter gave a small shiver. "Yeah. Or Wolf will. Wasté kte sni." *It won't be good*.

"You can say that again," was Michael's glum reply to Peter suddenly switching to Lakota, the Native American language that Wolf that been teaching them for years. It just seemed to fit.

At that solemn reminder of possible consequences, Peter stuffed the note paper into his backpack. "We'll figure it out. Let's go to the Tiki Room. Like you said, we'll have to sit through the whole show."

"I like the Tiki Room."

"You would," Peter mumbled under his breath.

"What did you say?"

"Nothing. You want a Dole Whip?"

As the boys turned and left the Arcade, they headed for the first entrance off the main hub of Main Street, Adventureland. The Tiki Room was the first attraction guests came to in that land, and had opened way back in 1963. With its Tiki God show outside the thatched Polynesian-style main building, and the singing birds and flowers inside, it was still a popular show. The whipped, frothy pineapple dessert, Dole Whip, served outside had an almost cult-like following of fans.

As Michael happily ate the frozen treat while they waited for the show to begin, they didn't notice the same man from the Penny Arcade slip into the crowd just out of their sight.

"**U**nd now we will show you a magic trick," Fritz, the parrot with a thick German accent was saying at the end of the show. "We will open the doors outside und the audience will disappear!"

With smiles on their faces, the audience filed out, some of them still humming the popular main song of the show.

When the last of the guests were gone and the cast member Anne was checking the room for any debris, Peter quickly jumped up on the padded bench next to the tiki totem pole Walt had indicated. He knew he had only moments. Michael was all ready to go ask the cast member a question to keep her occupied—and turn her away from Peter—if he had to, but she seemed to be wiping up some spill on the floor. None of them noticed the man crouched down behind the last row of seats on the opposite side of the room from the boys.

Peter reached up to pull down the shut mouth of the tiki with one hand and insert his other into the hole. He found it was deeper than he would have thought. His fingers closed around something small and plastic and he had to give it a good tug.

"What are you boys doing?"

Peter dropped the capsule into Michael's waiting hands as he jumped down from the bench. "Oh, I was just seeing if the mouths moved on their own. That's all." As if to demonstrate, he put his hand on the lowest face and tried to move the mouth.

"Stop! Don't do that! They are very old and shouldn't be messed with," Anne told him, holding up her hand to stop him.

"Found it!" A male voice suddenly called from the other side of the room.

Three surprised faces turned toward the unexpected sound as a man stood from his hiding place. "Dropped my pen," he proclaimed with a huge smile, holding up the pen he himself had swiped from the Emporium earlier, hoping they didn't notice that the price tag was still wrapped around the blue stem. "You boys ready to go? Sorry if they were causing trouble, ma'am," Todd smoothly said as he walked over, putting a hand on their shoulders. Feeling them tense at a stranger touching them, he hoped they wouldn't start yelling or bolt. Talking fast, he added, "I thought I told you guys not to touch anything. Ah, you know how boys are!" He quickly guided them out of the open doors and onto the back porch of the building before the cast member could reply. Immediately removing his hands from their shoulders and taking a step away from them, he had already dropped one of the listening bugs he always carried into Peter's backpack before the boys could run off. He wanted to know exactly where they were so he could find them again and see what they were up to. From what he had just heard and witnessed, he knew they had to be involved somehow with Walt Disney. And that had to be worth a *lot* more than random wallets and purses. Holding up his hands in pretend innocence, he figured he needed to apologize for touching them. "Sorry, guys. I didn't mean anything by it, and you looked like you could use some help." Todd could tell Peter and Michael hadn't recognized him. If he had been in his security uniform, it might be a different story. But, for now, he was unknown to the boys and that suited him just fine.

"Uh, thanks, mister. We were just messing around. We need to go find our dad."

Little liar, Todd smiled to himself. "Sure thing, kid. Just be careful where you stick your hands."

He watched as the two boys ran off to the right and ducked into the Frontierland entrance. From there he knew they could go anywhere in the Park and, if it weren't for the well-placed bug, he'd never be able to find them again. Whistling "Let's All Sing Like the Birdies Sing," Todd looked around the busy entrance into Adventureland. There were guests heading to the Jungle Cruise or Indiana Jones, or just walking through on their way to Pirates of the Caribbean. Some were shopping in the Bazaar or deciding to try out the show inside Aladdin's Oasis. Leaning against the bamboo-like railing of the Tiki Room, Todd took his time fitting a small earpiece so he could listen in on where the two boys went. Enjoying the shady spot, he delayed heading back to his assignment on Fox Patrol, this time in Critter Country, as a pleased smile played across his face.

Back on Main Street, a different security guard was standing inside the Penny Arcade. Arms folded across his chest, Wolf stared at the Mutoscope. His sharp sense of smell could distinguish the faint aroma of ammonia over the more-enticing smells of vanilla and chocolate coming from the Candy Palace next door. Wolf knew what that tangy smell meant. One of Walt's clues had been seen and destroyed. Just to make sure, he quickly inserted four pennies, one right after the other, to see if the mechanism would trigger the clue. Just as he thought, only Charlie Chaplin appeared before his eyes.

Kimberly had alerted him early Thursday morning that the capsule inside the Golden Horseshoe had been removed. She had told him it was odd because it had happened the same day her family had been in Disneyland, but she didn't know the exact time of the extraction. Wolf had found no clues in the private booth on the second floor of the saloon. None of the cast members on duty when Wolf got there had been working the Wednesday shift, so no one had anything stranger to report than hearing some kid had slid down the banister that day. And now, just moments ago, she had called Wolf again. This time it was about the red light showing the clue in the Penny Arcade had been set off.

Wolf was just ready to leave the Arcade when his walkie-talkie beeped once more.

Glancing at the number, he saw it was the private line. Quickly glancing around, he saw he wouldn't be overheard. "Yes, boss?"

A feminine voice chuckled. "You don't have to call me that, Wolf!" Kimberly told him.

"Sorry. Habit." Wolf had worked closely with her father, a Guardian in his own time, and still missed him.

When Wolf said no more, Kimberly smiled to herself. Wolf wasn't big on small-talk. She got right to the point. "What did you find at the Mutoscope?"

Wolf looked back at the ornate machine. "I can't really dust it for fingerprints since it has been in use for months since the remodel of Main Street. But, there is the smell of ammonia, so we know Walt's clue was seen and destroyed, just as Walt designed it to happen."

"Do you know what the next clue was? Did Walt ever tell you?"

Wolf nodded, and then realized she couldn't see the gesture through the walkie-talkie. "Yes."

When she realized that was all he was going to say, she prompted, "And…."

"I was there when he filmed it. It leads to the Tiki Room."

"Ah, that explains it."

Wolf silently waited for her to continue. When she didn't, he knew it was her attempt to get him to converse more. Giving a half smile, he knew he could stand there all day. Giving in this one time just to speed things up, he asked, "Explains what?"

Her slight chuckle showed he was right. "The red warning light just went off in the Tiki Room."

"On my way," was Wolf's immediate response as he took off in a run towards the Adventureland entrance.

"Wolf," Kimberly called through the walkie-talkie.

"What? I'm almost there."

"You do know what this means, don't you?"

Wolf's eyes never stopped scanning the crowd. As he rushed towards the exit of the Tiki Room, he passed one of his fellow security guards currently working undercover. Giving the man a brief nod as he ran by, he curtly answered, "Yes, I do. Over and out."

The back porch of the Tiki Room was empty. Whoever had been inside the show had already filed out with the last group of guests. Standing on the second step of the exit stairs, Wolf stood still and let his sharp gaze fall on everyone within sight. There might be someone holding a gray capsule, or someone reading a small piece of paper, or someone looking overly excited for just walking through Adventureland.

Nothing. His searching eyes saw no unusual activity. Just hundreds of guests going to and fro, examining Park maps, and heading for their own adventures.

Disgusted with himself, Wolf picked up his walkie-talkie and pushed the button that went directly to the War Room. No other security guard had that button—only the original Guardian, Wolf. "Missed him," was all Wolf said and killed the link before Kimberly could start chatting with him.

Yes, he knew what this meant. Somebody was on the trail of Walt's Hidden Mickeys. Someone was following the clues Walt had laid out and all that it meant. Wolf reflected back to when someone else had been involved in Walt's adventure. It had been Adam Michaels and Lance Brentwood who were involved in a similar Hidden Mickey quest several years ago. And just a little while afterward, Lance and Kimberly were involved in one when Lance was told by Kimberly's father that he had missed a clue when on the quest with Adam the first time.

This time, though, it was different. Wolf had no idea of who it was who had found this important first capsule.

CHAPTER 4

It took most of Wolf's considerable restraint to keep from growling in frustration. He had been over and over the Golden Horseshoe's private upper box. He had gone over every inch around the Mutoscope in the Penny Arcade and had thoroughly examined the Tiki God in the Tiki Room so many times that the cast members working the show wished he would go elsewhere—no matter how intriguing the women found the silent, mysterious man.

I must have missed something, Wolf told himself for the millionth time. *But, what?* He stood, hands on his hips, staring at the unmoving tiki totem pole. He had even, much to the dismay of the cast member Anne watching from the edge of the room, stuck his fingers into the mouth of the upper face, just to make sure the capsule was actually gone. He knew what had been placed inside the mouth. He knew where it would lead the finders if they were sharp enough to figure out the clue. Having personally assisted Walt in this limited, focused Hidden Mickey adventure, he knew all he would have to do is just watch the next step to find out who it was who had discovered the clues.

But, that wasn't the way Wolf worked. He liked to be one step ahead of everyone else. And, more often than not he was successful. There had to be some clue left behind to identify who had stumbled onto this mystery. He just couldn't see it.

As the next group of guests filed into the colorful, bird-filled room, Wolf strode out the rear door—much to the relief of Anne who had been warily watching him. Anne had been on the receiving end of Wolf's investigation since she had been the cast member on duty when the capsule was found. The only details she could remember were a couple of kids playing with the tiki's mouth and their dad who immediately came to get them and apologized for their actions. She had described them as typical boys with light blondish-brown hair, aged anywhere from seven to fifteen. Their dad had on a loud Hawaiian shirt and also had brown hair, only darker than the boys. Medium height, somewhat strong looking, but a little over-weight. She hadn't seen the boys actually take anything, just one of them had been up on the bench fiddling with the mouth. And, yes, it had happened before. Kids like to play with the mouths that they see moving one minute and then still the next. Sometimes they poke at the eyes that move back and forth during the show, too.

Every time Wolf questioned Anne, the answers were the always same. He knew that was all he would get out of her.

Two boys and their father. Discoverers of the clue or just two kids messing around? In the Golden Horseshoe, he had been told again about some boy sliding down the banister on the day the clue was discovered there. Another boy? Or one of the same? There was no mention of a father figure that time. Unrelated incident?

Standing outside the Tiki Room, just off to the side where the handicap elevator was located, Wolf paused and leaned on the wooden railing. Thinking back to when he had worked with Walt and had promised to keep his legacy going, he wondered how this quest would turn out. There had been two major discoveries so far. The first involving Lance and Adam was where they had actually found Walt's long-lost diary hidden in Disneyland. Watching over them had been Kimberly's father, a year before Kimberly actually found out what was going on. Always watching from the shadows, Wolf had kept to the background on that Hidden Mickey quest. Kimberly's father had been in control as befit a Guardian of Walt.

That quest had taken a surprising turn when Adam and Lance had gone in different directions. Adam had made a significant find and was content. Reuniting with a former love, Beth, during the hunt, they soon married and were none-the-wiser to the larger, more important discovery Lance had made.

When it was necessary for Kimberly's father

to step in, Wolf was put on the alert. He even briefly partnered with Lance when Lance was told he had missed something the first time around. Just observing and enjoying the show Lance was inadvertently creating for him, he eventually bowed out and Lance found another partner—Kimberly. At her father's death she was suddenly thrust into a position of power that she had just started to understand.

Both of those new Guardians still worked at Disneyland to keep their eyes and ears on what was going on at all times. Lance was still a security guard and Kimberly now worked with the new cast members who portrayed the princesses who would greet the guests. She had been working as Belle when she and Lance first met. Now, mother of three boys, Kimberly worked part time and still loved going into the Park whenever she was needed.

Wolf thought Walt would like his new Guardians. He would have appreciated Lance's quirky sense of humor and he would have loved Kimberly's keen intelligence and knowledge of Disneyland. Plus, Walt would have liked the continuity of Kimberly carrying on her father's work.

Giving a brief sigh, Wolf realized that he really missed his boss. He had been with Walt for many years before Walt suddenly passed away in 1966. Knowing Wolf was a man with deep secrets and strange abilities, Walt always knew his legacy would be safe with Wolf in charge.

Walt was one of the only ones who had known Wolf's real name was Sumanitu Tanka which meant wolf in his native tongue. Taking up the name Mani Wolford when it became necessary, he was known by all others as Wolf. His Lakota heritage gave him a strong sense of completion and thoroughness. That was what made it so frustrating for the dark-haired, powerful security guard. Having loose ends like he now had in this situation was not something Wolf enjoyed or appreciated. Nor was being patient.

But, patient he had to be until he had something solid to go on. Knowing where the clues next led, he would just have to watch and wait. Knowing human nature, he knew whoever it was who had discovered the clues would not just sit on them. They would act eventually.

And Wolf would be there waiting.

Undercover again on Fox Patrol, Todd adjusted the small earpiece in his left ear as he patrolled the shops in New Orleans Square. He had been listening to Peter and Michael for almost an entire week now, trying to find out just what it was they had found in the Tiki Room. The surveillance equipment he used was state-of-the-art and had a tremendous range. It was the best that other people's money could buy. Even though he knew where the Brentwoods lived, he figured it would be pushing his luck to be seen skulking about outside their house. It was much more convenient—and safe—to just listen in with the bug he had dropped into Peter's backpack.

But, as he was finding, these were ordinary

boys who did ordinary things—constantly. Along with school that Todd had to listen through, there were also their friends and family that came and went as they came into range of the bug in Peter's backpack. Hoping the boys would have had a more focused attitude toward the exciting discovery they had made, Todd found that they seemed to have a short attention span when it came to what they had simply called "the capsule." He knew it was stashed under Peter's mattress along with some unnamed items they had found in the Golden Horseshoe.

Todd gave a small chuckle as he was stealing some tip money from an open receipt book on the table outside the French Market Restaurant. His unexpected sound turned a few heads of the guests sitting at the surrounding tables and he was required to put the money back. "Oops, dropped it," he smoothly said as he returned the twenty to the leather binder and walked off. *Idiot*, he chided himself when he had gone over to Café Orleans to try again. The way to be successful was to *not* draw attention to himself.

Bringing his mind back to his previous line of thought, he knew he was skilled enough to break into the house in the hills. But, breaking and entering was risky. And Todd Raven was all about reducing his risk factor. Hence, the long— the interminably long—hours he spent listening to the on-going drivel from the two boys and their friends. At least the backpack belonged to the oldest boy. That one could at least keep one line of thought going longer than his younger brother

Michael.

From what Todd was gathering, the family was expecting visitors this next weekend and they might all go to Disneyland together and have lunch Saturday afternoon at Club 33, the private, exclusive restaurant above the streets of New Orleans Square. Todd glanced up at the intricate wrought iron railings around the balconies of the posh club. He had never been there. Apparently all of the Brentwoods were members. Todd gave a snort of disgust. *Must be nice*, he grumbled, wondering how Lance had managed that on a security guard's salary. *Must be inherited*, he reasoned as he recalled what their house—their mansion, he corrected—looked like. Perhaps he should rethink his non-breaking-and-entering policy….

"Hey, Peter, you want to come over tonight? We have a new movie we're going to watch," Todd heard a young voice say over the roar of the bus. Why did the kid have to sit in the back next to the motor every stinking day? That roar was driving him crazy.

"Hey, Jason. No, I can't. I have to do some…umm, homework tonight."

"It's Friday! You can do it on Sunday like I do," Jason suggested, and then added hopefully, "It's rated R and my mom and dad won't be home. Stevie, Rob and Megan are coming over."

Todd could hear a long pause. Apparently Peter was thinking about it. "No, I really can't. I really have to do a bunch of research before tomorrow. But, thanks for asking."

"Aw, you're no fun." Apparently the disgusted Jason went to sit somewhere else because Todd didn't hear him again.

Once the bus dropped Peter off at his stop and he walked the rest of the way home, Todd could hear the same things he had been hearing all week: The front door slamming; his mother telling him not to slam the door; Peter asking what was there to eat; his mother asking him if he had any homework; Michael asking Peter to borrow something; the youngest boy, Andrew, vying for attention from all of them; Kimberly shooing them upstairs to do their homework; Michael asking for a dog yet again—even Todd was tired of hearing it; Peter dropping his backpack onto the floor or the bed; papers being removed from it; grumbling about teachers and unfair homework assignments; the computer being started up; Peter playing some game for about half an hour until Kimberly called up for him to do his homework; a chuckle from Peter….

Already knowing what the next two or three hours would produce, Todd was about to pull the earpiece when he heard Michael come into Peter's room, apparently uninvited.

"Hey, you're supposed to knock."

"I did knock."

"I didn't hear you, Michael. Go out and do it again."

"I'm not going to knock on your door again! That's stupid!"

"Shh, or mom will hear you, Michael. Did you finish your homework?"

"Why do I need Mom when I have you

telling me what to do?"

"Fine. I'm busy. What do you want?"

Michael was silent for a minute. "You missed a target," he offered.

"Where? Oh, thanks."

"Petey, Dad said we're going to Disneyland tomorrow with the twins and Uncle Adam and Aunt Beth."

"I know," Peter cut him off. "Get out of my room."

Used to this bantering they always did, Michael ignored him and just continued with what he had come in to tell his brother. "Do you think we can open the capsule now? Maybe it's a good time to see what we might have to do next."

Todd expected to hear Peter tell his brother off again, but was surprised when Peter agreed with him. "Yeah, I was thinking that, too. We might be able to go off on our own again with the game book and see what we find next."

"That's a good boy," Todd mumbled as he stopped next to the dock of the Tom Sawyer Island rafts. "Open the capsule, for crying out loud."

"What do you think it is?" The excitement in Michael's voice could be clearly heard through the earpiece.

Peter's voice took on a kinder tone than he had been using. "I don't know. It's pretty cool what we got from Walt so far. How about if you come back to my room after dinner? Ask me for help with some research you need to do. I'm sure we'll get plenty of time alone to look at it and try to figure it out."

"Oh, that's a good idea! Dad always wants you to help me with my schoolwork!"

Apparently Michael had turned to leave the room when Todd heard Peter call to him. "Hey, Mikey, quit with the dog already. You aren't helping. Give it a rest. You can bring it up again later. Okay?"

Michael's returning groan was heard fading away. Peter got up to slam his door shut and then immediately yelled out an apology to his mom. "Sorry, Mom, I didn't mean to slam it."

Todd finally pulled the small receiver out of his ear and tucked it into his shirt pocket. Smiling as he headed into Critter Country, he knew he had a lovely four hour break from listening to the incessant chatter from the Brentwood family.

Then, he hoped, he would get some long-awaited answers.

"This is really weird, Michael," Peter commented as he turned the paper over in his hand, a frown wrinkling his forehead.

Michael was busy examining the oddly shaped key and Mickey Mouse watch that had been stuffed into the small oval capsule Peter had pulled from the Tiki God. The key, according to what Peter had found online, was called a skeleton key. Brass in color, it had two fancy teeth that curved out from the carved shaft that was rounded on one side and perfectly flat on the other. The hole at the top of the key caught the boy's eye as he was sure it looked like a Hidden Mickey, only the ears weren't just exactly right.

The watch was smaller in size than what the boys usually wore. The leather band looked old, but the face of the watch was still in excellent shape. Mickey had a pointed nose on his smiling face and his two white gloved hands would have gone around the black Roman numerals if the watch had still been running. Peter had found an imprint on the back that read 1940 and guessed the watch had been made in that year. What the boys didn't know was that this watch didn't require batteries and they would have just had to wind the small stem on the side to get it running again.

Michael looked up from their discovery at his brother's words. "What's weird, Petey?"

Peter held out the yellowed paper that looked just like what they had found the first time. Michael didn't take it from him. "It looks like a clue," Peter continued when Michael refused the paper. "But, a part of it is crossed out. See here?" he pointed, holding up the scribbled note. "The words Grand Canyon are crossed out and the words Lilly Belle are written in above it. But, what's funny is that it doesn't look like the same person wrote it, from what I can tell." He shrugged and turned back to his computer. "I don't know. I'm trying to find a link between the two but can't."

"What if you tried them separate first?"

"Yeah, that's a good idea. I'd better try that. I'll start with Lilly Belle since it was written last."

"Can I see it again?" Michael asked, coming

over to Peter's desk. He carefully set the key and the watch next to the computer screen. With some difficulty he made out the clue: **Take a ride in the Lilly Belle. Careful where you sit. Don't get poked!** He gave a chuckle. "It says 'don't get poked' like you might sit on some-thing sharp. That's funny!"

"Yeah, funny," mumbled Peter, not really lis-tening. He had added the words 'Walt Disney' to 'Lilly Belle' in his search and came up with a lot of computer hits. "Hey, Mikey, look at this. The main thing the words Lilly Belle points to is a train. Over and over again, see? There was this little one that Walt had in his backyard, but the article says the house was torn down after the Disneys moved out. The train Walt built was called the Lilly Belle, but it is now in…," he pulled up another link and read for a moment. "San Francisco. Oh! We saw it when we toured the Family Museum there. Remember? It was about a year ago. Dad had the weirdest look on his face when he was telling Mom about the train. I never did figure out what he meant."

"We have to go to San Francisco? Where is that?"

Peter stopped and looked at his brother in disbelief. "You don't remember where San Fran-cisco is? We were just there a year ago."

Michael just shrugged, unconcerned. If he waited long enough, Peter would just tell him.

"It's up north, I don't know, about 7 hours or so from here. Took forever to get there. But, I don't think we need to go there. That train was really small and Walt would ride on it. All the pictures of this train show people sitting on top of the little cars with Walt as the conductor." He picked up the small piece of paper on his desk. "Look here at the clue again. It says we have to ride *in* the Lilly Belle, not on it like these people…."

"I'd like to have a train in my yard," Michael interrupted as he sighed wistfully, watching picture after picture of Walt's elaborate backyard train set scroll past on the computer screen.

"Yeah, but your dog would mess it up," Peter kidded, then he perked up. "Hey, look here at this link to Disneyland. This looks good. It says the Lilly Belle is a train car that only dignitaries get to ride in."

"What's a dignitary?"

"What? Oh, someone very important. Here's a picture of the outside of the car. Wow, it's really fancy. I wonder how we would get into that."

Michael's attention wandered back to the clue. "Why is Grand Canyon crossed out, do you think? Is that important?"

Peter tapped a few keys on the computer. "Well, since the Lilly Belle seems to be a train, let's see if the Grand Canyon is a train, too."

"That's not nearly as pretty as the Lilly Belle," Michael commented when Peter came up with a matching link. "What does it say?"

Peter read to himself for a few moments, scrolling down through the long article. "The Grand Canyon was built way back when Disneyland first opened. It was supposed to be a special train car for important people to ride in. They called it an observation car but when the dinosaur diorama was added—I always like that part—it was too hard for people to see out of the small windows. Plus, it took too long to load and unload, so it was put into storage in 1974."

"Wow, that's a long time ago. How are we supposed to ride in that?"

"Hold on, I think the story keeps going," Peter explained with a few more clicks of his mouse. "See here? Someone rescued that Grand Canyon car and wanted to turn it into something called a Presidential Car instead. That happened in 1976. After that, it was restored again in 1996 and again in 2005."

"Uh, this might be a dumb question, but Uncle Wolf told us Walt died in 1966. So, if Walt died, how did he put a clue in that train ten years later?"

Peter turned away from the computer screen and stared at his brother—who was obviously waiting to be told it was a dumb question. "You're right. I didn't think of that, Mikey. That isn't dumb."

He picked up the clue again and tried to think it through. "What about this? Maybe Walt *did* put the clue in the Grand Canyon car. But look at the note again. That was scratched out and the word Lilly Belle was written in by someone else. So, maybe somebody working for Walt moved the clue after he died, fixed the name of the train and put it into the Lilly Belle after it was built. It was the same train car, after all. Does that sound right?"

"Why else would someone scratch out

Walt's clue? That makes sense to me," Michael shrugged. His eyes moved back to the watch as he wondered if he would get to keep it.

"Then, who else knows about the hidden clue? If someone did move it for Walt, are they still watching to see what happens to it?"

Michael's head spun back around, his eyes wide. "Do you think someone knows we took it? Are they going to come after us?"

"I don't know, Mikey. I wish we could ask Dad about this, but he wouldn't understand."

"What do you want to do, Petey?"

Peter turned back to the computer screen and stared at the elaborate, mahogany-lined train car. "I think we need to figure out a way to ride in the Lilly Belle and see if something is still hidden inside it. Maybe we can get Alex and Catie to help."

Michael just nodded. He trusted Peter and knew his big brother would figure it out. He just hoped they wouldn't get into too much trouble this time.

CHAPTER 5

"It's a puppy!" shrieked Andrew and Michael at the same time.

Standing in the doorway of the Brentwood home, Beth Michaels looked very pleased with herself. Her twins, Alex and Catie, were almost bouncing up and down in their excitement to give their best friends one of Sunnee's puppies.

"You shouldn't have, Beth," Lance told his dear friend dryly. "Really. You shouldn't have."

"His name is Kevin!" Andrew suddenly announced.

"I'm afraid this is a little girl dog, honey," Beth explained with a smile, ignoring the look Lance was giving her.

"Then she is going to be Dug!" was Michael's declaration.

"Hope that isn't prophetic," grumbled Lance apparently to himself as no one was paying him any attention.

Always eager to please, Andrew took the name change in stride. "Maybe you can teach her to talk!"

All of the kids yelled, "Squirrel!" at the same time and started laughing.

The delighted puppy, the center of all the attention, wiggled her little tail, promptly piddled on the marble entryway and bounced over to sniff Kimberly's shoes.

"Really," Lance repeated to Beth, his eyes narrowed at the widening puddle, "You shouldn't have. Right, Kimberly?" he turned to his wife to back him up.

"Oh, look at that widdle cutie face!" Kimberly cooed, picking up the wiggling golden puff ball and cuddling it to her chest.

Lance, knowing he was beaten, just sighed and glared at Beth. "So, where's Adam?" he asked in a deceptively pleasant voice, adding under his breath, "So I can kill him."

Hearing what he said, Beth gave him a mischievous grin. "Oh, he had to work today. I'm sure you remember Rose Anderson? She wanted her bedroom remodeled again. She asked about you, by the way. Adam wanted me to ask if you wanted to join him on the job," Beth added, her eyes sparkling with amusement.

Lance almost choked at the mention of Rose's name. Adam had been doing work on her house when the two of them were on their first Hidden Mickey adventure. Rose was…. Lance shook his head. Rose was someone he wanted to keep a wide distance from—especially during a bedroom remodel. "Tell him thanks for the offer, but I think I'll pass. Now, about the dog…." He broke off when he saw the animal in question was being bundled out the back door to the play area.

"You mean Dug?" Beth asked with a wide innocent smile.

"Yeah, Dug…. Don't look like you're enjoying this so much, Shrew," he bantered with her.

"Grumpy," she shot back.

"Meddler."

"Pooper Scooper."

"All right, you two," Kimberly broke in, laughing as she reentered the house from the back yard. "You two will go on all day like that! Well, we got Dug settled. I think she likes it here," she said brightly to her not-so-charmed husband.

Lance rolled his eyes. "I thought we were all going to Disneyland today. We did have a plan, you know," he pointedly shot at Beth.

Smiling complacently back at him, she replied, "Oh, we can still go. You'll just need to build a little pen for Dug."

"I want to stay with the puppy!" Michael, who had been anxiously listening, yelled from the back porch.

"Me, too," Andrew and Alex chimed in.

"We have a reservation at Club 33 at two o'clock," Lance reminded everyone. "It was short notice and we shouldn't cancel it."

Peter and Catie hadn't given their opinion yet. After a moment of animated whispers between them, Peter told the adults, "We'll go to the Park with you."

"Well, we can't leave the other kids here alone. Lance, why don't you stay and knock up some kind of shelter for the pup until we can do something more permanent, and Beth and I will take the two kids to Disneyland."

Lance stared at his wife as if he couldn't believe she was not backing him up. Catching Beth's wide grin out of the corner of his eye, he sighed dramatically. "Fine. You go. Have fun without me. I'll be fine. No really," he held up a hand, "I insist. Go."

Without another word, the four went running out the front door and piled into Beth's Jeep. Before they could take off, a back window rolled down and a large bag of puppy kibble was dropped onto the gravel driveway.

As Beth and Kimberly chatted in the front seat catching up on all their news, Peter was catching Catie up on his own news. After getting an okay from Michael—who seemed relieved that someone else knew about their little secret—Peter told Catie about their finds at both the Golden Horseshoe and in the Tiki Room.

"But you can't tell your parents," he quietly stressed. "At least not yet. Mikey and I want to see how far this takes us before we need to tell them."

Catie nodded her head. She was a miniature version of her petite and pretty mother. At age eleven, she seemed older than her twin brother Alex, and Peter was glad it was she who had wanted to come along. "We have four more puppies just like that at home," she had told Peter in explanation of why she wanted to go to the Park with them and not stay back to play with the pup. Thinking on what he had just told her, Catie could see the excitement in Peter's green eyes. She nodded again. "Yeah," she whispered back. "Mom and Dad would never understand the excitement of finding something like that. They're too old!"

"Okay, here is what I think we need to get done today. We need to ride in the Lilly Belle to see if there is another capsule or something hidden somewhere in the car. I didn't bring the clue to show you," he told her, "but it mentions not getting poked. So, I'm thinking it is something down in one of the chairs. In the pictures they all looked really padded and soft."

Knowing Disneyland almost as well as her mother, Catie frowned as she thought. "But, Peter, not just anybody gets to ride in that car. It's pretty special and might not even be out today."

A quick look of shock passed over the boy's face. Peter's mouth formed an O, and then shut. "I didn't think of that," he admitted. "What will we do? We *have* to get inside it."

"You sure you don't want to ask your dad? Mom says he can charm the scales off of a snake!"

"Really? Hmph, wonder why she would say that? No," he decided, looking out the window as Harbor Boulevard whizzed by as they neared the Park. He knew Beth would veer over to Disney Drive soon and head for the huge parking structure. "No, we can't tell my dad yet. Do you think your mom could do it? She's worked there forever."

Catie contemplated the suggestion. "She does get to work on whatever she wants to because of all those Disney artifacts she loaned to them. But, I don't think she'd be able to pull that off."

They were both silent as Beth ran her employee I.D. card into the parking lot scanner. The arm swung up and she steered through the structure, looking for a spot close to the elevators. Since it was Saturday and apparently very busy already, she ended up two floors higher than she wanted. "Should have parked in the employee lot," she grumbled to Kimberly as they piled out of the Jeep.

"No problem," Kimberly smiled good-naturedly. "We aren't in any hurry. Are we, kids?"

Heads together again, Peter and Catie didn't hear them. Their moms, seeing their preoccupation, gave each other an encouraging grin. They always hoped the two would remain close friends as they got older and more mature—a thought that would have produced an "Ewww," from each of the ones under consideration at this point in time.

"Wolf!" was heard by the moms.

"Did you say wolf?"

"Um, Uncle Wolf. Is he working today? I just wanted to ask him something," Peter turned a hopefully-innocent looking smile on his mother.

Her green eyes narrowed, she just replied, "I don't know. If he is in the Park, I'm sure he'll find us."

Kimberly and Beth exchanged a mom-look

as the two kids ran ahead to the escalator and headed down to the trams for a ride to the main entrance. "We'll probably never know," Beth sighed to her friend.

"Not if they don't want to tell us, that's for sure. And Wolf won't be any help."

"I haven't seen Wolf in quite a while," Beth commented as they took a seat on the crowded tram. "How is he? Any new girlfriend? He's how old now? Thirty?"

Kimberly just smiled and kept silent as the tram whisked them through the winding turns of the private drive alongside Disney Drive. Wolf had been thirty for as long as she had known him. That was one of the mysteries of this particular Guardian.

"**W**olf! What are you doing here?" Kimberly asked, wondering why she was surprised when their friend suddenly showed up beside them at the door to Club 33 on Royal Street. She had just been ready to push the call button when she felt an unannounced presence beside her.

Dressed in his security uniform, Wolf nodded his greetings to Beth. They had met years ago when she was working on the Pirates of the Caribbean ride, shortly after Adam's and her hunt had concluded. Wolf had been looking for the missing Lance and wondered if she knew where he might be. Now, since all of them were friends again, he fell into the couple's company often. "Lance called and told me you needed another person for your reservation. He was grumbling something about a dog, but I really wasn't listening. If you don't mind, that is," he nodded to Beth.

"Théhaŋ waŋčhíŋyaŋke šni, Uncle Wolf!" Peter told him, obviously happy at this turn of events.

"Long time no see to you, too. Very good, Peter. Tókheškhe yaúŋ he?"

"I'm fine, thank you," Peter replied, always pleased to show off his Lakotan to friends.

"All right, you two," Kimberly smiled. "Let us in on the conversation, too."

"Sorry, Mom," Peter mumbled. Glancing over at Catie, he threw a look at Wolf using only his eyes and then smiled knowingly at her.

Realizing what he meant, she gave a small nod. Maybe now they would find out about the Lilly Belle.

It was now apparent that the lunch would turn into a pleasant two hour respite from the rest of the day. Beth and Kimberly, both members of the Club, enjoyed the unhurried meal. Peter and Catie enjoyed the elaborate dessert table. Wolf, as always, just ate whatever was put in front of him.

When Kimberly and Beth went off to the ladies room, Peter saw his chance. "Uncle Wolf, can we ask you something?"

Getting something of a grunt in response, the boy continued. "Do you think you can get us onto the Lilly Belle for a ride? We've never been on it."

The corner of Wolf's mouth turned up briefly. It was as close as he came to smiling. "Most of the millions of people who come to Disneyland have never been on it," he told him as he tried another sip of the mint julep Kimberly had insisted he order. He gave another grimace and set it aside, shaking his head.

"I know," Peter insisted, looking down the long entryway to see if his mom was coming back yet. Wolf caught the look, but didn't say anything. "But, it would mean a lot to us," indicating Catie as if that would help, "to get to ride it. Do you think you can arrange it? Today?" he added, hopefully, his eyes wide.

Wolf gave an inward smile. Peter was unconsciously turning on the charm just like his father did. "Is it that important?" Wolf asked, seeing Peter glance down the hallway again.

"Yes!" Catie and Peter claimed at the same time. "We really need to go on it."

Wolf gave a small shrug. All he had to do was make a call using the number on the Guardian's private line. With its voice-scrambling technology, the person at Disneyland answering the call wouldn't even know who it was who was calling. They would just know they had to do whatever was asked. Wolf rarely used the line. He left that to Lance or Kimberly as befitted the ones who took over her father's role. Looking at the eager faces and hearing Beth's voice as the women came back toward the table, he gave a short nod. Holding up a hand so they didn't start whooping in delight, he added, "I'll see what I can do."

Catie looked so pleased Wolf was afraid she was going to try and hug him. Getting quickly to his feet, he told the returning women, "Meet me at the Main Street train station at 4:30. I have a surprise for all of you."

Used to his abrupt comings and goings, Kimberly just nodded. "Sounds good." She looked warily at the two eager, young faces in front of her. "You know what this is about? You two look like you are about to burst."

"You're going to love it, Mom!" Peter promised. "Can I have another piece of cake, please?"

Kimberly let her son distract her. She would find out soon enough what this was about. "Sure, honey. Help yourself. Catie? You, too?"

Both of the kids walked quickly to the dessert table and picked up fresh plates, their heads together again in excited conversation.

Beth glanced over at Kimberly, who too, was watching them. "Great plans are in the making."

"Yes, I can see that. We'll find out around 4:30, I'm sure. Want to tease them and say we have to be home by 4 o'clock?" Kimberly asked with a wicked grin.

"Oh, that would be so mean! I love it! But, no, let's see how it plays out. I'm curious now. Especially with Wolf in on whatever it is."

The Main Street Train Station was a charming building built to look like a depot in the early 1900's. Inside the small station was an assortment of artifacts from the early days of train travel. On the wall was a large poster of the five steam engines that traveled around the Park.

Wolf was waiting for them at the left side of the loading area, near where the back of the train would stop. Peter and Catie had to restrain themselves from actually running towards him and jumping up and down. He wasn't fooled by their slow walk in his direction.

"Are we on time?" Kimberly asked, looking around at the other guests waiting patiently for the next train to arrive. It was pretty busy that late in the afternoon. She could see over the tracks to the main entrances of both Disneyland and California Adventure. There were still a lot people streaming into both parks.

The recorded announcer proclaimed that the next train was arriving. Right on cue, they could hear the bell ringing and the chug of the engine as the *C. K. Holliday* pulled past them, the engineer waving at the guests. With a screech of the wheels, the stately train came to a stop with an explosion of steam up in the front. The conductors immediately got to work and ushered departing guests towards the exit and opened the gates for the new passengers to board.

James, the conductor with the most seniority, came to greet Wolf and his party. Wolf hadn't let the curious women enter beyond the gate. As they looked toward the back of the train wondering what the delay was for, Kimberly and Beth both let out a surprised gasp. The Lilly Belle was standing ready as the last car.

"If you will follow me, please," James tipped his hat and led the party to the end of the platform. Reaching into his vest pocket, he pulled out a small brass key and fit it into the highly polished lock on the front of the bright red car. "After you, ladies." He held out his hand and assisted Beth, Kimberly, and Catie into the plush interior. Peter and Wolf followed, all of them taking a moment to let it sink in that they were actually inside the most exclusive car in Disneyland. "Enjoy your journey," James tipped his hat again and, reaching out an arm, signaled 'all aboard' to the next conductor. The signal was transferred up to the engineer, and the *C. K. Holliday* gave two short whistles to indicate she was ready.

As the party inside the mahogany car found seats, Kimberly finally found her voice. "How did you do this, Wolf? This is amazing! I never thought I would be traveling in the Lilly Belle!" In the excitement of the moment, Kimberly forgot that she, too, as a Guardian, could have arranged a trip in the special car.

Beth was too stunned to say much of anything. She ran an unbelieving hand over the cool marble surface of the round table next to her claret mohair-covered couch. Ignoring the 'Please remain seated at all time' warning heard through the sound system, she wandered over to one of the walls to look at the picture of Walt and his family framed there. The lace curtains in the windows fluttered in the breeze coming through the open windows. She glanced up at the twelve stained-glass panels that were lit overhead. "This is absolutely stunning," she whispered to no one in particular.

Peter and Catie appeared to be too excited to sit still. They bounced from one of the seats to the next, not staying in one chair very long. The thirty-seven-foot-long car had seating for fifteen people, so they had plenty of choices for seats. But, they didn't appear to like any of them.

Wolf, standing in the back of the car near the curved exit door, had been casually looking out the back window. But, the actions of the two kids finally caught his attention. While it might look like they were too excited to sit still, he knew Peter better than that. There seemed to be a purpose in what he and Catie were doing. He saw their hands slip behind them as they sat and disappear a ways into the mohair cushion.

His mouth slightly fell open as he covertly watched them. They were searching for something. It became too obvious to him. When the train neared the ToonTown station, they stilled their movements and remained in one place. But, once the train got moving again, the previous actions were resumed. They were trying to be random, but he could tell they were hitting every seat in the car. He chuckled to himself when Peter suggested his mom try a different chair to see how comfortable it was just so he could search the seat she had been sitting in. Catie tried the same with Beth. When Catie reached back into Beth's vacated position, her face gave a momentary look of shock, which she managed to quickly cover over. Motioning for

Peter, he came to sit next to her. Only Wolf saw the transfer of the gray capsule to Peter and it being dropped into his backpack.

Peter was one of the boys who found the clues! Wolf had to keep from staring at the boy who would have surely noticed, his mind spinning. Two boys had been in the Tiki Room. *I'll bet anything it was Peter and Michael.* There had been one boy reported sliding down the banister in the Golden Horseshoe. *Probably Michael covering for Peter while he retrieved the first plastic canister,* Wolf silently worked out to himself.

Putting a thoughtful hand to his chin, Wolf continued to stare out the back window as the last white spires of It's a Small World disappeared around a carefully trimmed topiary hedge. He had never thought it would be a child who found Walt's trail of clues. He gave an amused grunt. Peter wouldn't like being called a child—and he certainly showed maturity in a lot of things. But, this? What would his parents think?

Glancing at the boy, who was finally content to sit in one chair, Wolf figured Lance—and Kimberly, for that matter—more than likely did not know about this find. Peter was too secretive, both in Club 33 and here in the Lilly Belle. What an interesting turn of events! The sons of the current Guardians finding the next set of clues. Wolf almost smiled at the thought.

Wolf liked the boy. He had always wanted to take him back to meet his family, but knew Peter's parents wouldn't allow such a journey.

Thinking back on the chain of events up to this point, Wolf remembered that the family had been in Disneyland each time the War Room system had been triggered. Why hadn't he seen the evidence before him? Apparently Lance and Kimberly didn't notice the incongruity either. Something would have been said. So, who was the mysterious man that Anne in the Tiki Room said had come to the boys' rescue when they were seen sticking their hand in the tiki mouth? She assumed it was their father. But, based on the evidence in front of him, it couldn't have been Lance. He was too well known in Disneyland. Should he ask Peter about it? Would Peter figure out Wolf knew all about the Hidden Mickey trails? Would he eventually conclude that Wolf was the one who had placed the clue back into the train car each time it was restored?

As the train pulled into the sparse Tomorrowland station, the Monorail was just pulling out with a double blast of its loud air horn. Peter and Catie rushed to the back window next to Wolf to see the sleek blue body slip by overhead and out of sight on its way through California Adventure and over to the Downtown Disney station.

So many questions and no easy answers. "Back to your seats," Wolf told them as the train gave a lurch forward to start on her journey through the Grand Canyon and Primeval World.

"You're standing," Peter started to argue until he saw the look on Wolf's face. "Sorry," he muttered as he took a sofa next to Catie.

When Peter started explaining to Catie how the Lilly Belle used to be known as the Grand

Canyon, Wolf knew the boy had been doing his homework and was in this for the duration.

On the alert now, Wolf would step back and observe—just as he had done in the years past.

Wolf wasn't the only one who was closely watching Peter's actions. Earpiece in place, sitting in the last row of seats in the next train car, Todd Raven was watching as best he could through the narrow windows. He could see that the girl had finally stopped bouncing from one seat to the next. When Peter came to sit next to her, only he heard her muffled voice say, "I found it, Peter! I found it!"

There was silence, and then the capsule actually hit the bug hidden in the bottom of the backpack, making a loud scraping noise against the microphone. Todd couldn't see Wolf at the far end of the train car. But, he knew he was there and, thanks to the kids' whispers, he knew Wolf had somehow arranged this special trip. What role did Wolf play in all this? He didn't know Wolf all that well on a personal level, but he knew enough to be wary of this particular security guard. He also knew Wolf and the Brentwood family were close friends. All of this meant he would have to tread very carefully from now on.

Todd smiled a smile that didn't reach his eyes when he turned back in his seat as the train tunnel that connected Tomorrowland and Main Street got darker and darker. When the opening strains of Ferde Grofé's "On the Trail" started playing, he didn't even look over at the vivid colors and beautiful artwork that made up the Grand Canyon diorama. He had more important things to think about.

He had some artifacts to steal.

CHAPTER 6

September, 1962

"Come in," Walt called when the little bell on his door inside Disneyland chimed. The doorbell always sounded like it belonged on a girl's bicycle rather than on the private apartment of one of the most famous men in the world.

A blond-headed man popped his face around the corner. "You ready to go to the studio, Walt? You have that promo for the Pirate attraction today." When he got no response, he stepped further into the room and worriedly added, "You okay, boss?"

Sitting on the sofa bed, Walt pulled his gaze away from the small kitchenette across the room. Turning to his right-hand man, he quietly admitted, "Yeah. I'm fine. Just a little distracted today."

"Anything wrong? You were pretty sick for a couple of days. We were worried about you.

That's why the doctor asked me to go to the Studio with you today."

"No, no," Walt waved off the concern obvious in the man's voice. "Not wrong, exactly. Just a strange dream, delusion, hallucination…I don't know what to call it…I had it again while I was out of it." Walt broke off, staring into the distance, thinking back to 1940 when he had first had that vision.

"Musta been some dream."

"Yeah, it was." Walt gave him a crooked smile, "You were in it, now that I think about it."

The blond man turned back from the entry door, his hand gripping the knob. "I was? Good guy or bad guy?"

Coming up behind him, Walt affectionately slapped him in the shoulder. "Oh, you're always a good guy." He paused as if considering whether or not to tell any more of the story. Thinking it would be good for a laugh, Walt decided to continue. "As a matter of fact," he said as they were slowly going down the stairs next to the Fire Station that led to the backstage area of Main Street, "you and Wolf were in charge of all of my affairs after I died."

"Really? Wow, that's something!" he laughed good-naturedly.

"You put into play this huge treasure hunt I had set up so I would be remembered. It was…it was quite involved." Walt momentarily stared off into space. 'Involved' seemed such an inadequate word to describe all he had seen.

The blond haired man gave his boss a friendly pat on the arm, bringing him back to the present. "Oh, you don't need a treasure hunt to be remembered, Walt. You'll live forever!"

Walt didn't reply as they got into the waiting car his doctor had also insisted on calling for him. Walt wasn't thinking about driving just then anyway. He was thinking of the phrase 'live forever' and the way the mysterious blond man had woven throughout his vision. Walt's attention came back again when his aide said, "Take us to the studio, Daniel, if you would. We're a little bit late."

"Right away, sir. Afternoon, Mister Disney."

"Afternoon, Mister Crain," Walt said automatically and then his eyes widened.

If the studio chauffer wondered why Mister Disney's startled gaze shot up to the rearview mirror after he returned the greeting, he knew better than to ask.

Walt sat off to the side on the set of his promo, waiting quietly until he was needed, his forgotten script hanging loosely from his hands. The vision he had seen again while he was sick was still strong in his mind as he watched people come and go, readying the cameras and the lights and setting the props in place. One of his long-time employees came and sat down beside him. "H…how are you today, W…Walt?"

The dream faded a little as he turned with a smile. "Jeremy! I was hoping you'd be here. How's everything?"

"G…good, thanks. Anything new and exciting going on, Walt?"

Walt rubbed the back of his neck. *I could use a massage right about now.* "You mean besides New Orleans Square, the Jungle Cruise, the Haunted Mansion, Mineral King, Aspen, Niagara Falls, and the World's Fair in New York? Naw, not much."

"Oh, good," Jeremy kidded back. "J..Just as long as you're not overworked! Say, they're al...almost ready for you on the set. It'll be an easy day today. I heard you were sick."

Walt gave the security guard a good-natured look-over. "You know, Jeremy, with your good looks, you should be in front of that camera instead of my ugly mug. I could make you an honorary Mousekateer or an ambassador! How does that sound? Then I wouldn't have to do these things!"

Jeremy gave a silent laugh. He and Walt always got on well. Walt never made fun of his stuttering. In fact, his boss always acted as if he never noticed it. "Well, I would, W...Walt, except for one *little* problem that I have," he smiled, holding two fingers up about an inch apart from each other.

"Problem? You, Jeremy?" Walt pretended to be shocked. "Why, everyone thinks you're just perfect."

"Yeah, hard to believe, huh? I t...try to hide it, but it's always there."

"And what problem would that be?"

Jeremy gave him a big grin. "I...I'm shy!"

Walt gave a hearty laugh and slapped Jeremy on the shoulder. "Well, we'll have to work on that. Say, where's your friend, John

Michaels? I need him to build something for my train at Carolwood."

Walt didn't think Jeremy heard him as the studio guard was smiling at a beautiful brunette who was approaching Walt. There was a clipboard in her hand on which she was slowly writing notations. "We're ready for you to take your place, Walt. Hey, there, Jeremy," she grinned almost, but not quite, timidly, her blue eyes sparkling. "Are we still on for tonight?"

"Absolutely, Dana. I'm looking forward to it. I was going to pick you up around six if that's a good time for you."

He was rewarded with a slow wink and devastating smile.

As the long legs sauntered off, Walt got up from his chair and nudged Jeremy. "Say, how come you don't stutter around her?" he kidded.

Jeremy looked back from admiring the view of Dana leaving. "I…I'm not sure. Maybe she scares it out of me!"

With remnants of his dream still floating around in his mind, Walt gave Jeremy a parting, mysterious smile. "You'd better hang onto that one, then. A man can always use a woman who scares him a little." Walt took a step away and then turned back to the security guard. "Say. Jeremy, let me ask you something. I didn't want to say anything in front of her, but didn't Dana used to work in Ink and Paint? I thought I had seen her in The Nunnery."

"Why, W..Walt! That's No-Man's Land. What were you doing there?" Jeremy gave a short laugh. It was common knowledge that

Walt preferred to have women working at the de-tail-oriented Ink and Paint Department coloring in the animation cels that would then be taken to be shot for whatever feature they were for. The Nunnery was a small break area between the Paint Room and the offices in which the women worked. Trying to keep distractions down to a minimum, Walt had declared the break area to be for women only—hence the nickname The Nunnery.

Walt waved off Jeremy's question. Every-one knew Walt went where he wanted whenever he wanted to go there—including The Nunnery. "It just surprised me that an Ink and Painter would switch to working on the sound stages."

"I, uh, I think they're waiting for you now, Walt," Jeremy glanced nervously at the set, not wanting to get Dana in trouble if Walt wasn't happy with her shifting assignments.

"Let them wait."

Knowing now he was expected to answer, Jeremy told his boss, "Okay, Dana had been in a car accident and it messed up her right hand pretty bad. I don't know if you noticed how diffi-cult it was for her to write." He broke off, hoping Walt got the point.

He had. A look of compassion crossed over Walt's face. He knew the women were proud of their work. It must have greatly bothered Dana to lose her position. "Gosh, that's terrible. Thanks for telling me."

"No problem, W…Walt. I'll send John over when I find him. I think he's working with the contractor in New Orleans Square today. Not sure, though. I'll have to tell him right away. He's getting married soon."

"To Margaret?"

Jeremy looked a little surprised. "W…why, yes. I didn't know you knew her."

In actuality, Walt didn't know Margaret. But, how do you explain about people you don't know but saw in the depths of a long, rambling vision? Walt gave a small grunt and shook off the images that were always right there in front of him. "Anyway, getting back to John, yeah, send him over when he can make it. He does beautiful work. Has he ever thought about running his own company?"

"Every day."

When he could see Dana coming back to get him, Walt said with a grin, "Uh oh, here comes the boss. I'd better get to work. See you later, Jeremy."

"Here, you go, Mister Disney. You need one of these if you're going to walk around in here."

"Thanks, Russell," Walt said as he accepted the hard hat, replacing his comfortable fedora with it. The worn wool hat was unceremoniously crushed into his jacket pocket as he tried to decide which way to go.

As the foreman walked off, Walt looked around the huge excavation site. He was excited about his walk-through Haunted Mansion attraction—even though there were many differing ideas on what should be included, both inside and outside the building. For some reason he couldn't understand, the developers were not that excited about his "Museum of the Weird Restaurant" he wanted to build next to the mansion. He had already gotten his way on how the exterior would look, though. It had been proposed as a run-down antebellum mansion with tall weeds and dead trees decorating the grimy exterior. The boss had finally put his foot down and insisted on a pristine white building. "We'll take care of the outside and let the ghosts take care of the inside," Walt had told them, ending that debate. Now the Imagineers were going back and forth on whether the scenes should be scary or funny. The mock-ups they had made in their WED Enterprises studio had been significantly frightening enough that the nightly cleaning crew—who walked in on the effects still running late at night—quit and told them to clean their own studios.

Still chuckling over that incident, Walt spied the person he wanted to talk to. "John!" he called over to the young, wavy-haired blond man consulting a set of blueprints.

Looking up, John was surprised to see it was Walt Disney himself who was waving him over. Getting a nod of an okay from the foreman, John set the prints down on a plank that was sitting on two sawhorses. His mind in a whirl, he carefully walked over the assorted steel rebar and electrical pipes that had already been laid out. His soft brown eyes seemed curious as he greeted the boss. "How are you today, Walt?"

"I'm good, thanks. I was just talking to your

friend Jeremy. He probably hasn't had time to call you yet."

John gave a friendly smile at the mention of his popular friend. Everyone knew Jeremy. "No, I haven't heard from him in awhile. He's probably busy with Dana, I'm sure."

"Well, I wanted to ask you about this little project I have in mind for my train back home...."

Nodding as Walt mentioned his favorite hobby, John wondered why the boss suddenly stopped talking and walked over to a stack of gray plastic pipe that had been unloaded off to the side while it waited to be installed. Watching, he was curious as Walt picked up a smaller length of what looked like a six-inch diameter pipe and began to study it closely. Walt next reached into his pocket and pulled out his car keys, dropping them into the open end of the thick pipe. When the keys came to rest against the secure end cap, Walt then lightly shook the pipe, carefully listening to the effect.

"Umm, working on some new sound effects, Walt?" John ventured a guess as he came up next to Walt.

"What?" Walt's eyes seemed far away when he turned to face the construction worker. Recovering quickly, he gave a small grin. "Oh, no. I was just...I just...." *I just realized this is the capsule that all the clues had been buried in...,* he was thinking to himself. Realizing he had stopped in mid-sentence, Walt held out the gray pipe he still have holding in his hands. "What is this, exactly?"

"That's the latest thing in electrical pipe.

This stuff is great and it's supposed to last forever. It's called PVC conduit. Comes in all sizes
and shapes. Whatever is needed for the electricians running wires through it. What you're holding there is a conduit. And these are the pipe
connectors," John pointed to a different stack,
"and those are the end caps, like the one already
on the pipe you're holding. When the pipe is
gray—like this batch—it's electrical conduit.
When it's white, it's used as underground water
pipe. The electricians will use glue to hold the
connectors and caps firmly in place, once they
are set." He wasn't sure how much more of an
explanation was needed as Walt continued to
stare at the short length in his hand, already having retrieved his keys from it. "Uh, did you want
to keep that?" John shrugged, not knowing what
else to say.

Walt handed it back to him, and smiled self-
consciously. "No, no. Thanks for the information. You're a General Contractor, aren't you?"

That surprised John. He hadn't thought he
had mentioned his goal to anyone on the job.
"Well, I'm studying to become one," he answered slowly. "I have to know *all* the trades to
be qualified to get my license. And that's what I
appreciate about working here at Disneyland. I
get to work in every trade."

Walt dusted his hands off on his slacks,
leaving two white smears. He seemed unsure
what to do next. He gave a final stare at the gray
pipe and raised his hand in a good-bye for John.
"Thanks again. Oh, by the way, congratulations
on your upcoming marriage."

As Walt carefully made his way back to the exit gate of the Haunted Mansion construction site, John just stood there staring at the retreating figure, his head slowly shaking side to side. Odd interview aside, it never ceased to amaze him how the boss seemed to know everything about everyone. It was then he realized Walt hadn't finished telling him what was needed for his train. Glancing up as the foreman came over to him, giving Russell the I-have-no-idea-what-that-was-about look, John figured Walt would contact him again when he was wanted.

Walt leaned against the railing on the drawbridge of Sleeping Beauty's Castle, facing the water and lost in thought. "It all started with a moose," he mumbled as his eyes followed a black-masked, white swan that sedately swam in the green water of the moat below. But before the beautiful bird could disappear under the arched passageway, it looked upwards at the man and gave a loud hiss. Suddenly flapping its wing, it came halfway out of the water, straight at Walt, startling him. Eyes wide, he whispered, "Rose?" as the swan sat back into the water, settled her ruffled feathers and, with a few strong kicks, placidly swam out of his sight. Heart pounding, he shook his head as he clutched a small black leather book in his hand, his knuckles white.

As he stood there lost with his thoughts, a tour guide, dressed in her trademark plaid outfit, walked by, leading her group into the Castle, and telling them the story of the Sleeping Beauty. At the sound of her pleasant voice, he remembered to turn his head away, pulling the brim of his fedora a little lower on his forehead to help hide his identity. There was so much going through his mind right then that he didn't want to be recognized or disturbed. Under normal circumstances, he would love to meet the guests and sign a few autographs. However, these were not normal circumstances for Walt.

Even though many days had passed since he had gotten over his illness, the images of the fever-induced vision were still strong with Walt. He was remembering the glimpses he had gotten of his Disneyland in what apparently was to be the future—his future, if he understood it correctly. There were some different rides than what were in Disneyland now, some attractions had been removed or changed, and he had gotten the impression that there may have also been another whole Park where the parking lot was now situated. *Wish I had seen more of that*, he mused to himself. *Maybe I can catch another fever or something to bring it back….*

With a chuckle at that nonsense, he made a couple of notations about the Haunted Mansion in the notebook he still held in his hand. When he closed the cover and was ready to slip it back in his pocket, he found himself staring at the black leather, his fingers slowly tracing a pattern over the soft front. If he had been asked at that moment what he was doing, he wouldn't have been able to explain. Then it suddenly hit him. *This was my diary in that vision*, he recalled with a sharp intake of breath.

"Is everything all right, Walt?" a low, deep voice asked, appearing to have materialized out of thin air next to him.

Startled by the unexpected sound, Walt fumbled. Eyes wide, he saw, as if in slow motion, his hands suddenly lost their grip and the little book arced upwards and then began to freefall. A dark hand instantly shot out and caught the diary before it had a chance to land in the water below. "Thanks," Walt mumbled, impressed by the quick reflexes. "I'd be lost without this little book!"

The journal was handed back to its owner. "Glad I was here. Is there anything you need, Walt?"

"No, no, I'm good. Thanks, Wolf," as Walt tried to keep from staring into the deep blue eyes of the security guard. "Is everything all right in the Park?"

As Wolf turned his head towards Main Street, his eyes constantly moving, his silver-tipped black hair brushed the collar of his uniform. He was the only man in the Park allowed to have his hair that long. For Wolf, people—even Walt—made exceptions. "All's quiet today. No problems to report."

Walt gave him a friendly slap on the shoulder. "Glad to hear it," he muttered and then drifted off. Becoming conscious of the man waiting quietly next to him, Walt suddenly added, "Say, Wolf, walk with me over to Tomorrowland, will you? I want to check something."

With a silent nod, Wolf complied, slightly curious to see what was wanted of him.

Walking in silence, Walt came to a stop in front of the eighty-foot-tall red and white rocket-ship called the Moonliner that stood at the entrance to the Rocket to the Moon ride. Staring up at it, he shook his head disgustedly and for some reason unknown to Wolf mumbled, "Pizza."

"You hungry, boss?"

He had momentarily forgotten the security guard was next to him as he recalled parts of the hallucination, the vision that plagued him and played back in his mind for twenty years now. "No," he answered with a covering, nervous laugh. "Just thinking," as he glanced over at The Flying Saucers ride. Moving on a cushion of air, the futuristic-looking saucers were a variation of the bumper cars idea and were just then being pushed back to the landing area by the long sweep arm. The attraction had a history of being on-again/off-again. But Walt wasn't thinking about the temperamental ride. The memory of the tall, white spires of something called Space Mountain overlapped the out-in-the-open Saucers that just happened to be working that day. "Hmm, a roller coaster inside a dark ride…. Is our future of 1985 wrong?"

Not sure if the question was for him or just random thoughts as his boss considered building something different for his Park, Wolf asked, "Planning something new?"

"Always," Walt muttered, almost too low to hear for anyone but Wolf. He glanced up at the well-known face of the guard. "You've been with me for how long? Forever, Wolf?"

The serious demeanor cracked into a rare smile. "Yeah, something like that, Walt."

"You're a good man," his boss murmured. With a far-away look in his troubled eyes, Walt turned to head over to New Orleans Square to look in again on the progress of the finishing work on the streets. Before he took two steps, he realized the security guard was still following him. Stopping in his tracks, he dismissed Wolf, adding sincerely, "Thanks again for my notebook."

Wolf just smiled as Walt walked off, head down and writing something else in the little book he had pulled out of his sweater's stretched-out pocket. The guard's sapphire blue eyes narrowed. "Don't worry, Walt," he muttered, watching until his boss passed through the fort entrance of Frontierland and out of his sight. "You won't lose that diary. It's too important."

CHAPTER 7

"Don't use the Internet. Don't use the Internet," Todd was chanting to himself as he listened in on the excited talk between Peter and his brother. "Call the girl on the phone, you pampered brat," he willed Peter.

Not knowing they were under surveillance, Peter was recounting the trip on the Lilly Belle to his somewhat interested brother. Michael was too distracted by the puppy he had snuck up the stairs, and hoped she wouldn't piddle in Peter's room.

"So, I need to let Catie know what I found inside the new capsule," Peter was saying, his voice getting louder as he neared the spot where he had dropped his backpack. "Hey, is Dug chewing on my sock?"

A low growl was heard as Michael tried to pull the black sock from the clamped jaws of the puppy. "She's stronger'n she looks," the younger boy muttered as he tugged. Sensing a new game, Dug lowered her head and shook the sock side to side, her plump rump high in the air, stubby tail wagging. Delighted, she gave a sharp yap which allowed Michael to free Peter's good sock. Promptly waving the sock in her face again, Michael laughed when she clamped down again and pulled backwards.

Peter gave a sigh. He could tell Michael didn't care about the new clue right then and he could also see that he was going to need a new pair of socks. "I'm going to see if Catie's online," he basically said to himself as he sat at his desk and pushed aside his homework.

"Dang it!" Todd yelled into the empty living room of his apartment in Brea. "Now how am I going to know where they go next? Stupid puppy," he muttered as the sound of growling could be easily heard through his earpiece. Apparently the game of tug-of-war had gotten closer to the backpack. In spite of himself, Todd smiled at the antics he could hear. He had had a puppy growing up. Tapping the side of the soda he was drinking, he idly wondered what kind of dog this pup was.

*A*re you there? Peter typed.

Just a sec. BRB, was the reply.

The 'sec' drug out to a couple of minutes as Peter stared at the cursor on his screen blinking on and off. *Hey!* he tried again.

Hey, yourself. Had to see what mom wanted. What's up?

Thought you'd want to hear about the next clue, he teased.

OMG! What is it? I've been dying to hear from you!

Peter smiled at the screen. He could see her face actually saying, "OMG." Not liking to type all that well, Peter tried to figure out how to say it in the least possible words. *Capsule smaller than first ones and had another key and note.*

What did it say????????!!!!!!!

Peter shook his head. Girls. *It said **Get Thee to the Nunnery. Bring a shovel and don't mess up the Ink & Paint**.*

IDK what that means.

"I don't either," the boy muttered to himself. *Have to do research. Want to help?*

Can I?????!!!!!! What do I do? I've never done this before. What about Michael?

Staring at the screen, Peter's hands froze over the keyboard. What about Michael? He had started this game with his brother, but now Michael seemed more interested in the puppy. Would it be all right to keep going with Catie now? She seemed eager to help and they had been friends forever. Peter glanced over at the antics still going on in his room. Now it looked like Michael was using the abused sock to blot up some piddle on his carpet. He shook his head and started typing again. *Ok for you to help. Mikey busy with Dug. See what you can find about Nunnery and Ink and Paint. Gotta go. Dug messed in my room.*

LOL!!!! Don't let your mom see! I'll get back to you later. TTFN. Catie.

What's TTFN? he wrote back, a quizzical

grin on his face.

Ta Ta For Now, ROTFL!!!!

Bye, he typed and logged off, his eyes still rolling. Maybe he should rethink using his eleven-year old friend as his partner now. "Hey, Mikey, it's okay if Catie helps me with the next clue, right?"

Glad he wasn't getting yelled at for the dark stain on Peter's carpet, Michael grabbed up Dug in his arms and started for the door. "I think she needs to go outside again. Uh, yeah, I guess. Did you guys find something?"

Peter opened his mouth to answer, but Michael was already out the door and heading down the hallway. Mikey's interest level didn't even include waiting for, or caring, about the answer to his question. When Peter heard Michael thumping down the stairs, he muttered to himself as he stared at the torn, smelly sock that was left behind in the middle of the room, "Guess I have my answer. Catie it is."

Repeating the way he had solved the mystery of the first clue, Peter started looking in the search engines again. He typed in 'Walt Disney Nunnery' and hoped for the best. As he started scrolling, his face fell. "I have to go to Disneyland in Hong Kong? How am I going to pull that off? No, it can't mean that. I don't remember Dad or Mom ever talking about Walt going to Hong Kong."

Not even wanting to consider that was the answer, Peter kept searching. He found links to a Disney movie that featured a nunnery, numerous people who had that last name, and more than a few people who were educated in convents.

Switching his search to 'Ink and Paint,' he was dismayed to find over five million results. "This is going to take a while," he groaned. He was onto page seven when he realized he hadn't narrowed the search down to 'Disney Ink and Paint.' "Hmmph, that's better. At least it is under a million results."

As he continued to scroll, he eventually saw something that recurred quite often, something that made him sit closer to the computer screen. "That's more like it. The Disney Studio."

Pulling up random articles, he found the clue could probably refer somehow to the important department of the Burbank Studio. He read how Walt liked to use women in that department because he thought they had a lighter, steadier hand at the delicate work than men. There were numerous articles highlighting different women who came to some prominence after getting a start in that department—including Walt's wife, Lillian. But, he couldn't find any reference to a nunnery within the Studio. Thinking it meant a place where nuns lived, Peter couldn't see a connection.

Looking back at the subject line he had typed in the search engine, he decided to run all the words together and see what happened.

To his delighted surprise, he scrolled down and saw his answer immediately. "That's what the Ink and Paint Department was called because of all the women who worked there! Bingo!"

Excited by his find, he kept reading and found there was a little side court between the Ink and Paint department and the Paint Room where all the colors were stored. Located across the street from the more prominent Animation Building, this court was also a No-Man's Land where the ladies could take their breaks and then get back to work. There were benches, a tree and a few bushes that lined the two buildings.

Looking at the bushes, Peter thought he knew what he needed to do. "Bring a shovel," he repeated. "I just need to dig up something Walt left there." His smile faded. "How am I going to pull that off? First, it's No-Man's Land, and second, don't you think someone is going to notice a kid digging up their flowerbed?" he asked himself, throwing his body back in the chair. He came up with one more problem. "How will I even get onto the Studio property in the first place? That's where the work is done, but I know it's not open to the public.... Wolf? No, I can't ask him for another favor so soon. He might get suspicious and ask what I'm doing. Mom? No, she only knows people inside Disneyland. Dad?" Peter paused and looked at his screensaver that had just clicked on. Images of their family's trip to Walt Disney World in Florida filtered past his unseeing eyes. He moved his head side to side as he pondered the pros and cons of asking his dad. Lance seemed to know everyone everywhere they went. But, Peter realized he'd better have a *really* good reason to ask his dad to drive him all the way to the studio in Burbank.

Logging back in, he decided to let Catie know what he had found. He anticipated a lot of exclamation points in her response.

"The Studio? In Burbank? Why does he need to go to the Ink and Paint Department?" Todd pushed the small earpiece further into his ear as if that would make Peter read him the whole clue out loud. "C'mon, kid, read me the rest of it. I know you can't get on the lot, too. Shoot. I should've grabbed his backpack once they got off the train."

Todd wandered into his kitchen as he listened, randomly opening cupboards trying to find something to eat. "Okay, out to dinner or go to the store? Out to dinner," he immediately decided, grabbing some money out of one of the wallets he had stolen. "Thank you, Mr. Enright," he chuckled as he tossed the brown leather back onto the pile.

Leaving in the earpiece, he headed for his parking space. As much as he was ready to grab the clues and take whatever treasure was at the end of the quest for himself, Todd was also beginning to view his voyeurism as a type of entertainment—almost like an ongoing soap opera starring people he actually knew. *Walt Disney and the Brentwoods* he saw as the title. *One man in the past and one family in the future. How will their worlds collide?*

Todd started chuckling as he put his older model Toyota in gear and backed out. "I should have been in advertising!"

Burbank – September 25, 1957

The camera panned back in the darkness and the eerie music faded away as a smiling Walt Disney could be seen in the one bright spot of light. As the darkness melted away, he raised his right arm to point at a wall of shelves and filing cabinets that were just coming into view. "Don't be scared," he admonished with a mischievous twinkle in his eye. "It's just me. You see, the name Morgue doesn't have to mean something spooky or dead. What we have here behind us are shelves and tables and file cabinets that hold the whole history of our motion picture studio!"

Walking over to the first low set of cabinets, Walt pointed out various props and set pieces from different movies. "We shot many great films here in the Studio," he continued. "*Pinocchio*, *Dumbo*, *Bambi*, *Cinderella*, *Peter Pan* and many others. And these," his arm swept in a wide arc, "are the models, sketches, drawings, storyboards, and backgrounds for every film we've made. This is all our experience, and experience is the key to progress."

The camera followed Walt as he walked under one doorway that had *Peter Pan* posted overhead. "As you can see, our Morgue isn't a place of death. Once we finished a picture, we had to make room for the next project. Everything we'd used for that story had to be put somewhere. So, this huge room beneath the Ink and Paint Building became the finished film's last resting place. It might house the ghosts of our Animation Past, but we hope that all our retired research and artwork will help inspire artists in the future to go on to bigger and greater work."

Walt walked back into the first room and gave the small globe sitting on a cabinet a spin. "Now let me introduce you to our first True-Life Fantasy," he said, clasping his hands together. "His name is Perri and this is the tale of the little guy's life in the forest. Take it away, boys!" With a small salute, Walt signed off with his trademark grin as the camera faded to black.

Fullerton

"**D**ad!"

Lance gave a moan. He knew that tone of voice. Peter wanted something. Slipping down a little lower in the leather chair behind his desk, Lance hoped Peter wouldn't see him in the slightly darkened office. No such luck.

"Dad, there you are. You hurt your back?"

Lance sat back upright and fiddled needlessly with the papers in front of him. "No, I'm fine. What's up?"

"You remember Mr. George?"

The name coming out of the blue meant nothing to Lance. "How many guesses do I get? Is it animal, vegetable, or mineral?"

"He's my history teacher, Dad! You just met him at the Parent/Teacher thing last month."

Now Lance had a face to go with the name. Mr. George was Peter's favorite teacher, probably ever. "Yeah, I know," Lance covered over. "What about him? You fail a test or something? You need me to go beat him up?"

Peter gave a cheeky smile. "I get A's in that class, and you know it. I really enjoy all that history stuff."

"Yeah, I know," Lance said again. He was actually pretty proud of all the extra assignments Peter did for that class. It would be interesting to see what his son did in the future with his knowledge of history. "So, what about Mr. George?"

"Well, you know Teacher Appreciation Day is coming up." Peter broke off when he saw his dad's eyes drift towards the calendar on the wall. "Next week, Dad, on Tuesday."

"Right. And…."

"And I wanted to get Mr. George something really nice. Something different."

Uh oh, here it comes, Lance thought to himself, managing to keep a straight face. "Different," he echoed. "What did you have in mind? How about a puppy?" *Worth a shot*, he thought to himself.

Peter tried to play it cool. "Well, I was thinking it should be something not everyone could get. Like a pen set or maybe a coffee mug from the Studio in Burbank."

Lance was not expecting that. "Um, that would be nice, Pete. But the Studio isn't open to the public. You know that."

"Yeah, I know," Peter nodded enthusiastically. "That's why it's such a good idea."

"The Studio isn't open to the public," Lance slowly repeated.

Peter gave him a smile that Lance immediately recognized. He had used it often enough himself. "But I figured you could do anything."

"That's laying it on a *little* too thick, Peter," Lance counseled with a sly smile. He studied his oldest son for a moment. "Is it that important to you?"

Sensing a victory was coming, Peter managed to keep his facial expression neutral and just nodded quietly.

Lance looked out of the window next to his desk. Michael and Andrew were playing with that puff ball of a dog again. It didn't help Lance's attitude toward the dog to know that the pup's mother weighed in at one hundred pounds. Bringing his mind back to Peter's request, he knew all it would take would be one phone call to any of his numerous friends who might be working at the Studio that day. He had a sneaking suspicion that Peter knew that fact, too. Still, Lance let his son sweat it out for a couple of hours. "Well, let me think about it and I'll get back to you."

Peter opened his mouth to say something, but wisely clamped it shut again. "Thanks, Dad."

As his son reluctantly turned and left the office, Lance gave a huge smile behind Peter's back. The moment Peter was out of sight and hearing range, Lance picked up the phone and dialed Norm at the Studio. It would be great to see some of his old friends again.

At noon the following Saturday, Lance and Peter pulled into the Buena Vista Street entrance of the Disney Studio. On duty in the small guard-house, Norm greeted the two Brentwoods and handed them white I.D. cards to clip on their shirts. "Long time, no see, Lance," Norm was saying after Lance had parked in front of the trailers of some celebrities who were filming at the nearby soundstage. Since it was the week-end, most of the stages were dark. "Where have you been? Everyone's been asking about you."

Lance leaned against the side of his Jaguar while Peter slipped on his backpack. "Dad!" Peter interrupted, correctly assuming that the two men were about to launch into a lengthy dis-cussion about all their mutual friends. "Can I go get a couple of pictures of the Roy and Minnie statue? It's in the Disney Legend Plaza. I'll only be a minute."

Looking to Norm for an okay, the guard just shrugged. "It's really quiet today. Only one tour going on and no filming. You going to have lunch in the commissary?"

Peter nodded enthusiastically. "Yeah, I'm starved!"

"You're always starved," Lance muttered with a fond smile.

"Like father, like son," coughed Norm and earned a grin from his friend.

"Okay, go ahead, Peter. Don't get in anyone's way. You know the way, right?"

As Peter ran off towards the main avenue behind the Animation Building, Norm commented, "Yeah, he knows. So, what brings you into our neck of the woods? What's new with the family?"

With his chin, Lance indicated the disappearing figure of his son. "He wanted to do some shopping for one of his teachers. And I thought it would be a good time to remind you about our party in a couple of weeks."

Norm's eyes lit up. "Your Annual Security and Princess Gala?"

"Well, that's its unofficial title," Lance laughed. Every year Lance and Kimberly threw a party for all the security guards and all the princes and princesses who worked at the Parks and the Studio. Going on all day and well into the night, the cast members could come and go as their work schedules allowed. With the added attraction of the women who portrayed the princesses in the Parks, it was a very popular party.

"That's a big Duh that I'll be there," Norm kidded as he led Lance into the commissary. "Want to get a cup of something before Peter gets back?"

"What's on the menu today?"

"I heard they have ahi tuna," Norm suggested with a pat on his stomach.

"Now we're talking," as Lance grabbed up a

cafeteria tray and headed for the 'Seafood Section.' Peter was on his own.

Once out of sight of his dad, Peter picked up his pace and sprinted down the empty avenue behind the Animation Building. His goal was somewhere inside the middle of the Ink and Paint Department. He just hadn't figured out how to get inside there yet. Snapping a quick picture of the statue of Roy Disney relaxing on a park bench with Minnie Mouse, Peter looked around the area. At the other end of the Plaza stood the original Partners Statue of Walt and Mickey Mouse. Just in front of Peter, the seven dwarfs were holding up the roof of the Michael D. Eisner Building. Snapping a quick picture of Dopey at the very top peak, Peter turned back to his dilemma. As he was thinking, the only tour group of the day was just leaving the far end, having just taken pictures of themselves standing with Walt and Mickey.

Hurrying, he caught up with them as he heard the guide say they would tour the Animation Building, the tunnels, and then they would go to lunch. Quietly falling in behind the group, Peter tried to blend in, happily noticing his clip-on nametag looked almost identical to theirs.

"No cameras, now," the guide Christopher was telling them. "Once we get down into the Archives and the Morgue, no pictures."

As the group trooped down a long, sloping corridor, Peter listened to the story of the original Archives and all that had been saved for future generations to see. He was disappointed to see a sign on the door that said the Archives was not accessible that day.   The concrete tunnel, spooky in its own right with low ceilings, miles of exposed pipes and ductwork, and closed doors to hidden rooms, had also been used in numerous shows. While a nice side benefit, the tunnel had been used for many purposes. Walt had wanted to preserve the campus-like setting of the studio so all the utilities had been put underground—something that was unheard of back in 1940. Plus, the tunnel had been a way to protect the freshly painted animation cels. No matter what the weather was like outside, the cels were protected while being transported through the tunnel from one department to another.

Peter's disappointment at the inaccessible old location of the Archives was short-lived as the guide brought the tour up the other side of the tunnel and down a corridor lined with offices. Most of the doors were closed as it was not a workday for most people.

"And this," Christopher was saying, "is called the Nunnery."

Peter couldn't believe it as they were led into the narrow break area. Next to them, only one office, its animation table lit from underneath, was occupied. The woman at work ignored the hushed talk of the tour guide and continued her detailed work. After everyone had time to look into the window of the Paint Room and see all the plastic containers of color lining the walls, Christopher led them back into the corridor. "Now we will head to the commissary and you will have just about an hour to eat and to shop in the Studio Store before the bus leaves."

Peter's mouth fell open. In his excitement, he had forgotten about buying a coffee mug for Mr. George. He would have to remember to do that once he was done in the Nunnery.

Hanging back as far as he could, walking slower and slower, it was unnoticed when he walked backwards and ducked back into the break area. A quick glance showed him the animator was still at work, oblivious to the outside world. While he was with the group, Peter had looked over all of the plants in the small area and decided to first check out the low-growing shrubs along the one wall.

On his hands and knees, out of sight of any window, Peter slowly and meticulously examined every bush, not knowing at all what he was looking for. He pushed aside the greenery and basically hoped something popped out at him. As he worked further towards the back wall, he was starting to think he had made a mistake.

Then, unknown to him, Peter saw what his dad had seen in his own quests: The initials **WED** etched deep into the wall near the base of the dirt and a small arrow pointing downward. His heart pounding with excitement, Peter knew those initials stood for Walter Elias Disney and that he had probably just found what he was looking for. Glancing around one last time to make sure he was still unobserved, he removed his backpack. He brought out a small folding shovel he had taken from the camping gear in their storage shed. Trying not to hurt the plants, he shoved the tip of the six-inch steel blade into the hard dirt and tried to be as quiet as he could.

"**W**hat are you doing? Why aren't you with the rest of the tour?"

Surprised, Peter jerked around and almost fell backwards over the bench right next to him. "I…I was just looking into the Paint Room when everyone left. Are they all gone?" he asked, trying to sound worried and lost all at the same time. "The bus can't leave without me! I…I don't know how to get home."

The artist, on her requisite break, looked at the worried expression on the boy's face. He had obviously just lost track of time. "If you go down that corridor," she pointed, "just keep going until the end. The buses are usually just around the corner. Do you need me to show you the way?" she helpfully asked.

"Oh, no, thank you. I can find it!" Peter gushed, hurrying out the door and not looking back. He held back from actually running.

With a shake of her head, the artist mumbled something about "kids" and sank down on the garden bench. Looking around, she couldn't see anything that would have been that fascinating to a kid.

As she returned to her desk, she idly wondered when the gardeners had been there to dig up the soil.

Peter almost ran into the commissary and

held up a Studio Store bag for everyone to see. "Got it!" he exclaimed in a voice over-loud for the circumstances.

Looking up from his chocolate cake, Lance wondered why Peter looked so flush—almost as if he had been running the whole time he had been gone. Which was considerable, Lance noticed as he glanced at the clock. "You okay, buddy?" he asked as Peter threw himself down in the cafeteria-style chair next to him.

"Yeah, I'm fine. Can I have lunch now?"

Lance glanced again at the clock. "You've been gone quite a while. I already ate."

When Peter's face fell, his dad relented and indicated for him to get a move on. Already knowing what he wanted, Peter didn't wait for him to change his mind.

While Peter was busy getting a couple slices of freshly-sliced ham, Lance peeked into the shopping bag. There was an item heavily wrapped in cushioned bubble paper that he assumed was the mug, plus he saw a few new pins for Peter's lanyard. As he pulled his hand back, his smile faded as loose dirt fell off the handle of the shopping bag. Unconcerned, he shrugged as he dusted the dirt from his hand and went back to his conversation with Norm.

CHAPTER 8

"**W**ow, it's another key!" Peter exclaimed as he set aside the contents of the new capsule and stared at the brass object in his hand. "And it looks just the same as the first one we got in the Lilly Belle." Setting the new key down on his desk, he walked over and thrust his hand under the mattress on his bed to retrieve the first key. "Gotta find a new hiding place," he mumbled when he finally located the elusive item. "Some of these papers are getting messed up."

Comparing the keys side by side, they did, at first, appear identical. But when he tried to nestle them together, he found something out. "Ah, the flat part is on the opposite side. This one has to be turned around to fit." Once together, he could see the antique teeth were exact matches and the two parts made a significantly thicker key. "Wonder why there's two of them," as he held up the shiny object in front of his eyes, as his gaze kept going to the Hidden Mickey cutout at the top. From the research he had done on skeleton keys, he could imagine a long tasseled cord hanging from the cutout. "Maybe there are two doors I have to find. Ooh, or two treasure chests! That would be cool!"

The idea of having to locate something else reminded Peter that he still hadn't examined the rest of the contents of the newest gray plastic container. This one was slightly larger than the one Catie had found stuffed down into the cushion in the Lilly Belle. Besides the key, there was also another note written on the same yellow-edged paper and a wallet-sized card of a thicker ivory paper that had been slightly rolled to fit in the tube.

Uncurling the thicker paper, his eyes widened in surprise as he read the ornate wording that scrolled over the card. The first words he saw printed in a faded brown ink were 'Gold Pass' and that the Pass would 'admit the un-named holder of the card and his party of five to Disneyland.' On the left, next to the word Disneyland was a blue and brown representation of Sleeping Beauty Castle. Below a blue line that underscored the castle and Disneyland was the year of 1960 and Walt Disney's signature written with a thick blue pen. In smaller letters under Walt's signature was the title of President. Peter could see a curling filigree design all around the edge of the card and around the words Gold Pass.

"Oh, looks like I got a free admission to Disneyland," he gave a small chuckle. "And I can bring five friends with me. Oh well, that's too bad. I'll think about that later." Because his parents both worked for Disneyland, he knew he could get into the Park whenever he wanted. But, he realized some of his friends who didn't have the same privilege might enjoy a free day. Tossing the uninteresting pass onto a pile of papers on his desk, Peter turned to the other sheet from the capsule that he hoped was more interesting and important.

The yellowed paper had been folded in half and, with his heart beating a little faster, Peter pulled the edges apart to see what new, exciting mystery would be inside and worthy enough to be buried on the grounds of Walt's own Studio.

"Two keys are better than one. You will find the location of the secret door under the harpsichord's keyboard."

"What the heck is a harpsichord? I wonder if these keys fit into it. No," he reread the clue and answered himself, "It says a secret door. Cool! That sounds like fun!"

Turning to his computer screen and entering the word harpsichord, Peter began reading, "A harpsichord is a musical instrument played with a keyboard, producing a sound by plucking a string when a key is pressed. The harpsichord was widely used in Renaissance and Baroque music. However, during the late eighteenth century it gradually disappeared from the musical scene with the rise of the piano. But in the twentieth century it made a comeback, being used in historically correct performances of older music, in newer compositions, and in popular...."

"Okay, now I'm bored," he muttered, rubbing his eyes. "Why didn't they just call it a fancy piano…. So, what does this have to do with Walt Disney?"

He could tell the article he was reading never mentioned Walt as he quickly scrolled through the rest of its many pages, bypassing many pictures of the antiquated instrument. Going to the top of the screen, he condensed his search by adding the word Disney. "You'd think by now I'd just automatically do that," he jibed himself with a shake of his head.

Leaning forward into the screen, his eyebrows went up as he saw result after result that listed Club 33 in Disneyland as the location of Walt's, or rather Lillian Disney's harpsichord. He wasn't too interested in the beautiful wharf scene that had been painted on the underside of the lid by the Disney Imagineers. "Hmph, we musta walked right past it when we were there for lunch," Peter shrugged. "So now the problem is," he muttered, putting his arms behind his head as he leaned back in his chair, staring up at the unhelpful ceiling, "how do I get back into the Club."

When he couldn't immediately come up with a solution, he amused himself by spinning around in his chair. On one pass, his eyes happened to fall on the wallet-sized card that had accompanied the clue and that he had unceremoniously tossed aside. "I wonder what the search engines will say about a Gold Pass," he smiled as he typed in the words, not really expecting to find any references for one free day at Disneyland.

It didn't take long for his 'isn't-that-cute'

smile to fade. The look on his face was replaced with one of an almost reverential awe. For what he held—very carefully now—in his hands was a lifetime entry into every Disney Park around the world that was personally signed by Walt Disney.

His hushed "Oh, wow," didn't even begin to cover it.

Carefully listening to the musing and mutterings coming from Peter through the hidden bug still secure in the backpack, Todd pieced the clue and the next location together. "Figures," he snorted, "the brat gets to go back to Club 33 again and I've still never been there. I'll have to jump him when he comes out—whenever that will be." He popped open a beer and put his feet up on his messy desk. "I just hope he calls his little girlfriend and sets something up soon. I'm getting tired of waiting."

Todd took a long drink from the opened can. "Wonder if I should shake things up a bit. Let him know he isn't the only one in on this. Might scare the brat into doing something stupid." Todd gave a lopsided smile. "Stupid usually means mistakes. He's had way too easy a time of this."

He could tell Peter was now typing on his keyboard. "Rats. Doesn't anyone use the phone any more?"

Staring at his own computer, Todd had an idea. What if he posted something anonymously on Peter's social page? He had found the page when he had first started stalking the boy, occasionally checking to see if Peter was stupid enough to post something about his finds at Disneyland. Much to Todd's annoyance, so far he was not. Maybe a private message would be better, he decided.

Thinking for a minute on what to say, he pulled up the popular social pages and logged in using one of his many aliases. The Axeman sounded nasty enough.

I know what you are doing. I know what you found. Don't think you can keep this from everyone. If you don't turn over the evidence to me, there will be consequences you will have to pay. And that goes for your little girlfriend, too. Reply to this immediately and then I will tell you what to do next. The Axeman.

Todd chuckled darkly to himself. "Ooh, that's good. I like the part about the girl, too. Now let's see if he is smarter than he looks," as he hit send and then sat back in his chair to wait for Peter's frantic reply.

We need to go back to Disneyland and into Club 33. Any suggestions? he typed to Catie.

Hi, Peter! How R U? I'm fine. How is school? was her reply.

"C'mon, Catie, I don't have time for this," he mumbled and started typing again. *It's all good. Listen, we have to go back to DL. I got another clue from the Studio. Do you want to go, too?*

That's good! We sold the last puppy yesterday. : (I'm going to miss having them all around. Did you have fun at the Studio? I've never been.

Peter actually growled. "I'm not trying to chitchat, Catie! Gosh!" *Studio nice. FOUND CLUE. NEED TO GO BACK TO DL. DO YOU WANT TO HELP ME?*

Gosh, U don't have to yell. Sure, I'd <3 to help. What do we have to do?

"That's more like it. I think…. I don't know what <3 means, but I'm not going to ask," he muttered to himself. *Sorry,* he typed, *but I don't have much time. I'm trying to come up with a way to get back to the Park. This is Thursday. If we can, let's try to get back on Saturday. I'll get us into Club 33, I think….*

R U going to ask your dad or Wolf?

Peter stared at her question. Was he? His email button pinged. *Just a minute. I got an email.*

'K

Peter read the message from The Axeman and tilted his head, his eyes narrowed. He hit the reply button. *Knock it off, Jason. You aren't getting my autographed baseball cards*, and hit send. *Back,* he typed to Catie. *Just a dumb note from a friend from school.*

LOL I get a lot of those. What about your dad?

Still thinking about Jason, Peter had no idea what she was talking about and he didn't want to look back at her previous message. *What did you say? Repeat.*

Oh, man…. R U going to ask your dad or Wolf for help?

"Oh." *Not yet. Let's see if we can do this on Saturday. Just us. Mom and dad busy with party coming up. You are coming, right?*

Wouldn't miss it!!!!! :) I'll bring my family, too, she kidded.

Duh, he typed and inadvertently hurt her feelings. He wondered why it took her so long to respond.

When she typed again, it was short and to the point. *Will let U know.*

"No flowers and exclamation points?" he frowned as he saw she ended the conversation and signed off. Girls. Never can figure them out.

Paris – 1964

"There, that's what I was telling you about, Lillian! Isn't it beautiful?"

Lillian Disney couldn't see where exactly her husband was pointing. "What exactly am I looking at? The painting? That lovely table?"

"No, no, even though I do like that table. Wonder if it's for sale…. No, I mean the elevator."

Lillian gave him a smile. "You brought me all the way back from shopping to look at an elevator? Why ever?" She could tell by the familiar gleam in his eye that he was really intrigued.

He took her gently by the arm and propelled her forward. "Come and see the workmanship of this beauty. Look at that brass! Look at that wood! What is it? Walnut?" as he ran his hand lovingly over the smooth surface. "Oh, pardon me," he stepped back when two dignified-looking guests of the hotel wanted to use the machine in question. He moved back in closer when the lift—as they were calling it—moved upwards. Craning his head, he watched until it was out of sight. "I want it."

His wife was also familiar with that phrase. "Will we be installing it in our house? We might need to add a floor or two," she chuckled as they went over to sit on one of the upholstered sofas in the spacious white and gold lobby to discuss it.

"What? Oh, that's a good one, Lil!" he chuckled as he looked off into the distance, obviously trying to figure something out.

Lillian became a little alarmed he might actually be considering it. "No, Walt, I was just kidding. Our house is fine just the way it is," she said firmly.

Turning back to see her concerned look, he reassured his wife, "Oh, I know! I was just thinking about that V.I.P. lounge for Disneyland that I've been considering. What they did in New York at the World's Fair for those corporation bigwigs was pretty impressive. You remember I told you about them?"

Knowing what he expected, she nodded. "And you want to do something similar."

Walt's expression turned thoughtful and serious. "Yeah, I do. I couldn't have gotten Disneyland built without all those corporations chipping in. I want to do something special for them. You know, as a thank you." His gaze turned back to the elegant elevator which had returned to the lobby floor. "And that would look wonderful in the lobby of my special club! Come on, let's ride it. Then I'll go see if it's for sale."

"Walt, wouldn't this statue of the little boy look pretty in that courtyard you are planning in New Orleans Square? He looks so angelic! Walt?"

"Hmm? Yeah, sure. Go ahead and have it shipped over."

"You aren't even going to look at it or ask how much it is?"

Walt's face looked like he was mentally a million miles away when he turned to see what she was actually talking about. "What did you say? Angels? No, it doesn't matter how much it is. You're right. Maybe somewhere up on that sweeping staircase Herb designed." As he continued to stare at the ornate statue, he began to appreciate more of the detail. Including the pedestal, the piece was about four to four and a half feet tall. The young cherub-faced boy was dressed in a fancy cut-away coat and had on lace-edged knee britches. Looking off to the side, he was holding some kind of flute with both of his hands. "I know, in that rounded nook about halfway up. That's just the place," as he drifted off, staring again out of the window of the antique store.

"What's the matter, Walt? You tired?" Lillian

asked, placing a worried hand on his arm.

Fondly patting the offered hand, he gave her a small smile. "No, I'm not tired. I'm irritated. I can't believe that hotel owner wouldn't sell me that elevator."

"Now, Walt, some people do tell you no," she reminded him. *Sometimes not nearly enough*, she silently added to herself.

"That they do," he agreed. "And it irritates me every time they do it. Unless, somehow, they are right. And this guy isn't right. I *need* that elevator. Hey, you know what?" he suddenly perked up, snapping his fingers at the thought. "I'll send over a team of engineers and they can make me a copy of it. Probably be cheaper that way, anyway." He paused for a moment and dug into the stretched-out pocket of his sweater. "Ah, here it is," he mumbled. Holding up something bright, he showed it to his confused wife.

"What in the world is that?"

"That's part of the finish on the elevator. I got a piece of the wood, too. That's how I'll get it just right."

Lillian was shocked. "Walt! You can't just take hunks out of things!"

Waving off her objections, Walt gazed at the brass chip. "Oh, no one will notice. I'll have the boys match it up and bring over something to fix it back up. It'll be fine." Problem solved, Walt's attitude perked back up.

Once the transaction for the statue was finished and the shipping instructions given, Walt and Lillian wandered back outside into the watery, waning light of a late Parisian afternoon. "Might rain," he said, glancing up at the sky.

"Do you want to go back to the hotel?"

After a last glare at the threatening clouds, he shook his head. "No, there're a couple more antique stores I'd like to see before we go in. Let me tell you a little more about my plans for the special club in New Orleans Square. I think I'll put in a private entrance in your angelic court-yard to our new apartment, too. The one over the Fire House is getting too small with the grandkids now. Don't you think a piano in the main hallway would add a special touch?"

"Piano? In our apartment or in your club?" She wasn't sure which rooms he was describing right then.

"The club."

"Oh, all right." Lillian thought about the pro-posed club and then shook her head. "From what you've told me, I think something a little grander would be in order."

"A grand piano?" he chuckled.

"No. What about this: A harpsichord!"

That wasn't what Walt was expecting. She could tell he was considering it. "That's a keen idea. Where do you think I could get one?"

It was Lillian's turn for a secret smile. "Tell you what, Walt. Let me surprise you for a change. I'll take care of the harpsichord."

"You will? Why, that's a deal," he patted her hand one more time.

As they walked on, heads down against the chill in the air, Walt painted a vivid, lovely picture of the Victorian elegance he had in mind for his exclusive club high over the streets of New Orleans Square. He described how the waiters would be dressed and how they would bring in the best chef they could find. Chandeliers, elegant drapery, huge mahogany side boards, intimate tables for two by the many windows and large round tables for visiting groups all fell into place inside the two main dining areas.

Passersby barely gave the older couple a second look as they slowly trod along the busy Paris street. Had they stopped and listened, they would have been transported through time and space all the way to Anaheim, California, fallen as they would have been under the spell of the World's Greatest Storyteller.

CHAPTER 9

"Using this game book as a decoy was a good idea, Catie," Peter told her as they hurried through Adventureland. "Your dad didn't seem too interested in running a quest against us. Did he give you any trouble about coming back to the Park so soon?"

"No. Mom had to work in Pirates today, so he was going to do something with Alex and me anyway. Hey, slow down a little!" the girl rasped out as she tried to keep up with the long-legged Peter. "I can't walk that fast!"

"Oh, sorry," he mumbled for an apology. "Just excited, I guess." He adjusted his stride and let Catie set the pace.

Catie looked a little anxious about what she was going to tell Peter next. "I…I, uh, I had to tell Alex a little about what we were doing," she admitted in a low voice.

Her words took Peter by surprise. Other than Michael, who no longer seemed very interested, he didn't figure on anyone else knowing.

After remaining quiet for a few paces, he asked, "What did you tell him? Do you think he'll tell your parents?"

"No, I just told him that you and I found something really cool, but it was a secret right now. I promised I would tell him later when we know more. I...I think he won't tell. He did ask Dad to take him on Screamin'. You know I can't ride that, so I think he was trying to help us by getting Dad into the other Park." She paused for a moment, not being able to read Peter's face. "Is that all right, Peter?" More than anything, she hoped she hadn't jeopardized her chance to continue working with Peter. She enjoyed it more than she was willing to admit—even to herself.

Glancing at her open, hopeful face, Peter gave her an encouraging smile. "Yeah, I think it will be all right. He did convince your dad to bring us to the Park today. Michael is still ga-ga over the puppy, so he didn't want to come again."

Relieved, her heart-rate began returning to normal. It had sped up when she thought she might lose her friend. Changing the subject as they walked past the entrance to the Jungle Cruise, she asked, "So, do you know how we're going to get back into Club 33 yet?"

Glancing to the left and right, Peter lowered his voice to answer her. "Yeah, I think so. It should be on record that we had lunch there a couple of weeks ago. I'm hoping that will at least get us in the door." He gave her a charming smile. "I might 'suddenly' have to go to the bathroom, so don't look surprised. That should get me upstairs while they're looking for your sweater."

Catie gave a deep sigh. "I hope it works. I'd hate for them to call Mom or Dad and get us in trouble."

"Or call Wolf," Peter muttered through gritted teeth.

Hearing him, Catie glanced up sharply at his face. "Would that be bad? He did get us into the Lilly Belle."

Heading up the ramp that went over the queue for Pirates of Caribbean, Peter looked out over the Rivers of America that formed the heart of Frontierland. Wolf had a love of this area of Disneyland that went deep. Peter didn't understand it completely, but he knew the mysterious security guard could often be found there. "Wolf," he started and then stopped. They wove around the numerous guests who were lined up for lunch at Café Orleans and those who were exiting the Pirate ride. "Wolf is very smart," he finally continued as they walked past the Blue Bayou Restaurant, nearing their goal of the doorway into Club 33. "I'm afraid he would suspect something if he found we were back inside the Club for no apparent reason. I'd rather not have to explain anything to him just yet."

"I'd rather have him on our side, not against us," his companion muttered, not totally agreeing with him.

"Not yet, Catie. Not yet."

Peter wiped the palms of his hands down his pant legs. He didn't usually get nervous, but found his heart beating faster as he looked at the ornate scrolled glasswork that proclaimed '33.' It was the only outside indication of the exclusive club inside and most people wandering by either didn't see it or had no idea what it meant. The door, painted a non-descript blue-gray, was locked from the inside. Peter cleared his throat and mumbled, "Here goes nothing," as he lifted the small brass panel on the left side of the entry door and pushed the brass call button hidden within.

When a female cast member answered and asked for the name of their party, Peter lowered his voice and said, "Lance Brentwood. We were here two weeks ago and lost something. May we come in?"

Not knowing his family's entire history, Peter didn't realize that just the name Brentwood itself would have been sufficient to gain entry into the Club. He heard a bright, "Lance! Come on in," and the buzzer sounded, unlocking the door.

Giving Catie a pleased grin, Peter unconsciously took her hand as they went inside the burgundy and gold foyer. His grin faded a little when Louise, the cast member on duty at the entrance desk, became confused, looking beyond the two children for Lance. "Who are you? I was expecting Lance…and Kimberly," she added as an afterthought.

"I'm Peter Brentwood, his son," the boy hurried to explain. "This is my friend Catie." He dropped her hand, briefly wondering how he got to be holding it in the first place. "We had lunch here a couple of weeks ago."

"Yes. I was here then," Louise told them slowly, her eyes narrowing. "What's this about? Did you want to have lunch again? I can't do that without at least one of your parents being here."

"No, no," Peter held up his hands and then pointed at Catie. Embarrassed to be brought forward like that, she turned a bright shade of red. "She thinks she lost her sweater and we just wanted to see if it was found."

Louise looked at the stricken look on the girl's face. Either she was really upset about her sweater or she was about to cry. Or both. "I can check with the servers and see if anything was found. But, lost items are usually sent to the Lost and Found Department. Do you know where you were sitting? Which table?"

"Uh, the round one in the middle."

Louise hid a grin. That described every table away from the windows. "I'll call the maitre…."

Interrupting her, Peter suddenly blurted out, "Can I please use the bathroom? Please?"

Glancing over, Louise noted the painful look on his face and thought to herself, *Boys*. Out loud she gave a tentative, "Sure. Just follow the stairs…. Oh, you know where it is."

In a flash, not waiting for her to change her mind, Peter took off up the heavily carpeted staircase. He would have liked to use the really cool elevator, but that would take more time. After watching the boy streak up the stairs, Louise looked back at the girl who gave her a timid smile and a shrug. "Okay then," Louise started, "Let me call about your hat."

"Sweater," Catie corrected in a small voice. She didn't like deception and would rather be waiting for Peter outside on Royal Street.

"Right. Sweater," Louise gave her a small smile. She wasn't sure if she believed the story and was testing the girl—who was probably the weak link if it wasn't true. Still, she picked up the old-fashioned black phone and rang upstairs anyway. "So, what color was it?"

Once out of sight of the main floor, Peter slowed his steps and turned to enter the long hallway that led to the dining room. He could smell the tantalizing aromas from the food being served for lunch and his stomach growled. Almost immediately to the left was his object in question: the harpsichord. Painted a soft cream color with pale blue accents, the sometimes-working instrument sat near one of the many windows. Its long lid was propped open, revealing the painted scene of an older, original New Orleans on the inside of the cover.

Not seeing anyone in the immediate area, Peter grabbed a pen and small piece of paper he had stashed in his backpack and dropped the pack on the floor. Getting down on his hands and knees, he tried to glace up under the keyboard as the cryptic clue had said to do. Seeing nothing from that uncomfortable angle, he glanced around one last time and crawled under the musical instrument. Turning over onto his back, he could now clearly see something painted on the bottom of the harpsichord. The words were written in paint about two or three shades darker than the original cream and would easily be missed if someone wasn't looking for them.

In his excitement, Peter wrote the words on the palm of his hand, carefully copying each letter as it was apparent it was not written in English. When he was done, he looked at his palm and wondered how long the ink would last. Locating the dropped piece of paper, he was almost done copying the words a second time when he heard something that almost made his heart stop:

"Hey, what are you doing under there?!"

Peter felt hands grab his ankles and he was unceremoniously drug out from under his place of concealment. He found himself face to face with two stern-looking servers and the maitre d'. Getting clumsily to his feet, he held up his pen. "Found it," he tried with a feeble grin.

Seeing a guest coming towards them, the maitre-d' quickly dismissed the servers. "I have this," he told them quietly, taking Peter by the arm and leading him back toward the stairs. "What is the meaning of this? You were supposed to be just using the restroom. This is not a play area and you were under a most valuable antique!"

Peter wondered if breaking into tears would help. By the look on the angry man's face, probably not. "I'm sorry," he started. "I...I was hoping to grab a dessert. I haven't had lunch yet and it all smelled so good." *It's not working,*

Peter, he told himself. "So, I took off my back-pack and the pen fell out and it rolled…I'm sorry. I didn't touch anything."

The maitre d' wasn't sure what to do next. He knew the boy's parents and knew their children weren't considered troublemakers. About to release the boy with a strong warning, he was surprised when a uniformed security guard came rushing up the steps.

Peter's eyes got wide when he saw the uniform approaching. Then, when he realized it was not Wolf, he wasn't sure if he should be happy or worried. This guard was unknown to him. The name on his nametag said Todd.

Wordlessly pointing for Peter to remain where he was, Todd took the maitre d' aside a couple of steps and told the man that he would take it from here.

The maitre d' hesitated, putting a nervous hand on the back of his neck. "Well, there was no harm done, Todd," as he, too, glanced at the man's nametag. "I was just going to scare him a little so he wouldn't try that again."

Todd tried to give him a reassuring smile. "No problem. You did the right thing. I'll take care of it before any of your guests see the scene he is creating. I've got the girl waiting downstairs. You can go now," he tried to say in an authoritative tone, but came across as nervous and bullying.

Not liking it, but not knowing what else to do, the maitre d' nodded and turned back to the main part of the restaurant. As soon as the security guard had hauled the boy down the stairs, and enough time had passed to get the kids outside, he called Louise at the entry desk.

"Louise, why in the world did you call Security? I did find the boy under the harpsichord and he said he just wanted some dessert, but there was no harm done."

There was a long pause on the other end of the line. "I didn't call Security. I thought you did. The guy almost beat down the door until I opened it. The poor girl was scared stiff."

"I'm not sure what to do now. Do you think we should contact Lance?"

"No, I'm sure Lance knows this guard. He knows everyone. Let's just let Security do their job."

He gave a sigh. "Kids. You never know what they're going to do next."

Louise had to agree. "Okay, then, I'll talk to you later. We're expecting a party of eight any minute now. I'll notify you when they arrive."

With that, the two errant children were pushed from their minds.

Todd had been listening in on Peter and Catie's day and couldn't believe his luck when Peter announced they would be going to Club 33 to follow the next clue. On duty that day as a regular security guard, he had turned his steps toward New Orleans Square just as soon as he knew that's where they were headed.

Hearing all that was going on in the foyer, he knew the boy was up to something. Even he didn't fall for that 'I have to go to the bathroom' line. And, once he heard that Peter had gotten caught, he knew exactly what he would do.

Now he had the struggling boy by the straps of his backpack. Holding the pack slightly up in the air, Peter was unable to gets his arms out of the straps and was now a hostage. Catie wasn't about to abandon her friend and, head down, followed meekly behind the angry security guard.

Once they were outside the Club and the door had safely clicked and locked, Todd looked left and right. To the right was the busy entrance to the Blue Bayou Restaurant and the crowded exit of the Pirate ride. To the left was the rest of New Orleans Square down Royal Street and Front Street. It was not as busy in that direction, so Todd drug Peter past the two entrances of one of the shops and forced him into the curved entryway of the secluded Court of Angels.

Once they were totally out of sight of the guests wandering through the quaint streets, Peter was unceremoniously shoved against a brick wall just past a little-used burgundy door. They were actually behind the curved blue staircase that was the focal point of the beautiful courtyard and, thanks to an abundance of potted trees and plants, out of sight of the windowed doors leading into the shop. Leaning in close to the boy's face, Todd demanded, "All right, you little brat. What were you doing under the piano? What did you find in there?"

"Harpsichord," Peter struggled against the straps, but Todd still held them at a higher level.

"Don't get smart with me," Todd warned him

with a shake. "I don't care what it's called. Tell. Me. What. You. Found."

"What makes you think I found anything?" Realizing he was making it worse by struggling, Peter stilled his movements. Trying to look un-interested, he nonchalantly cast his eyes over-head. Because he was beyond the edge of the blue balcony on the second floor, his glance hap-pened to fall on the ornate stained-glass sign hanging up above him.

"I know everything you do," the guard hissed. "Ah, I see you don't look convinced. You!" he suddenly shouted at Catie who as start-ing to edge away. "Sit your little rear end on the edge of that pot and don't move another inch or pretty boy here gets it," pointing at the potted palm tree that was within his sight.

Not totally understanding what he meant by Peter 'gets it,' she took no chances. She didn't see any weapon, but that didn't mean there was-n't one. Scared and fearful of any harm that might come to Peter, she did as he said and perched uncomfortably on the edge of the clay pot, glaring at the man holding her friend cap-tive.

"Now, back to you," he shook the straps causing Peter's head to smack against the wall again. "I know you rode the Lilly Belle and found something. I also know you went to the Disney Studio and dug something up. Ah, I see by your eyes that you believe me now," Todd smiled a smug grin. "I want to know what you found just now in Club 33. Or, I can beat it out of you," he added with another shake.

"You wouldn't dare. Not here," Peter spat back at him, his brave words covering over his erratically beating heart. "There're too many people."

Todd didn't look too concerned and smirked, "Who said it would be here? I can get you backstage so fast even your girlfriend here wouldn't see it. So, let's just keep it friendly…. Tell me what you saw. Now."

Peter knew there was a cast-member-only exit just a few feet from where he was being held. He was also aware that the area behind New Orleans Square and bordering the Jungle Cruise wasn't a very-well used area—which made him even more nervous. Any cast members who went in that direction were usually on their way to the employee restaurant, The Pit. Quickly going through his options and not finding many, Peter decided to tell the truth. He didn't want this weirdo to even look at Catie. "I don't know what I just found."

There was excitement that came into the security guard's eyes. "Ah, so you did find another capsule. Hand it over."

"No. Ouch! Quit shaking me!" Peter tried to protect his head, but couldn't move his arms. "There was no capsule. Only words. But I couldn't read them."

"Liar. What did they say?"

Peter rolled his eyes and again saw the sign hanging over his head. His eyes widened a moment before he snapped his head down. "I told you I couldn't read it. It didn't look like English."

Todd looked confused now. "What do you

mean it didn't look like English? What was it?"

Peter tried to shrug, but his uncomfortable position wouldn't even allow that movement. Todd, seeing the movement, assumed the boy was trying something and banged him against the concrete again. Catie saw Peter's head snap back and she gave a small whimper, her hands curling into fists. Quickly looking around for anything she might use to help Peter, she saw only potted plants going up the stairway that would be too heavy for her to lift. Even the bordering shops seemed empty of people who might look out and come to their help—if they could even see them behind the staircase.

"Oww! I only know some Spanish and it wasn't Spanish. I...I wrote it down. It's in my pack," he sounded defeated and let his head hang down. He could tell the man holding him was thinking...and relaxing his grip. A possible plan came to Peter and he said to his upset friend, "Don't worry, Catie. I'm okay. It's just like Blind Man's Bluff. Okay?"

Her head came up and she stared at him. That was the name of a game the kids liked to play at the Park. They would take turns hiding and the others had to find them. She could see his eyes move quickly towards the exit on the right. Then his eyes moved to the entrance where Todd had drug him in. She hoped she understood what he meant. Giving him a brief nod, she leaned forward on her precarious seat and waited.

"Quit talking. This had better not be a bluff, or you are really going to get it," Todd told him, only half listening. Trying to come up with a solution to his immediate problem, he knew he had to get the backpack and get rid of the kids. There was an abandoned room under the Hungry Bear Restaurant he knew about. But, that was too far away to drag two kids, one who was getting angrier by the second and could do anything. He had to get rid of them quick. As two shots from the Jungle Cruise came faintly to their ears, he thought of another place. No one would find them for a couple of days. Peter didn't like the smirking look that came into the guard's eyes.

Coming to a decision, he hauled Peter away from the wall. "You two are coming with me. No noise or the girl gets the next treatment." He made a grab for Catie's arm. The position loosened his tight grip on the backpack and Peter suddenly raised his arms over his head. This angle allowed him to slip down out of the confines of the straps.

"Now, Catie! Run," Peter yelled as he turned, shoving the guard in the chest as hard as he could.

Taken by surprise, Todd's free arm was flailing as he tried to regain his balance. To his dismay, he watched as Catie shot out of the exit to the other end of the Courtyard and Peter took off straight ahead through the entry corridor.

The frightened girl ran straight to the Haunted Mansion and blended into the thick crowd at the entrance. Ignoring the looks given her by the guests already waiting in the queue, she inched forward step by step until she was near the front of the line. She gave a sigh of relief as the cool darkness of the ride's interior surrounded her. As the doors of the Stretching Room closed behind her, her erratically beating heart began to slow to its normal pace.

Remembering something Catie had mentioned earlier, instead of running straight through Orleans Street and into the crowd milling through the shops, Peter turned right and ran down Royal Street, veering into the exit of Pirates. Up the angled ramp, he quickly wove his way in and around the exiting passengers and melted into the flickering darkness.

Back at the entrance to the Court of Angels, a furious Todd looked left and right, unsure of which kid to follow. Somewhat out of shape, he seriously doubted he could catch either of them in a sprint. But, when he saw Peter angle towards the Pirate ride, he turned and followed.

"Got you now, you little…."

Working as a loader, Beth Michaels was surprised to see a flushed Peter hurry onto the exit dock. Not stopping what she was doing, she kept one eye on him while she helped a boatload of guests out of the flat-bottom ride vehicle. When everyone was safely off and the next passengers on the other side of the dock began stepping down into the launch, she went over to Peter.

Giving him a nice smile, she wondered why he kept looking over his shoulder. "You okay, honey? Where's Catie? Is she coming behind you?"

"We're playing Blind Man's Bluff," he told her a little breathlessly. "Any chance I can get in the back of this boat? Please?" he begged with a smile, unknowingly turning on his inherited charm.

Beth gave a smile. She would have liked to take a picture of his face right then to show his dad. It was like looking in a mirror. Familiar with the game that the kids liked to play, she knew one key part was that the players had to 'hide' by riding the nearest ride. Using walkie-talkies that they all would be carrying, they would have to give hints as to which ride they were on. The player who was 'It' would have to listen to the clues or the sounds coming through the speaker and wait for the one hiding to come out of the exit. If whoever was 'It' didn't figure out which ride the players were on by the time the ride ended, he was still 'It.'

Giving a good-natured chuckle, Beth held up a hand to signal the loaders and pointed to the empty back seat of the second boat. "Catie must be 'It,' then," she deduced. "Hurry and jump in there. And don't tell her I helped you! That would be cheating!"

Peter instantly relaxed once he sat in the smaller back row. He gave her a more natural smile. "I won't. Thanks, Aunt Beth."

Beth signaled to the Tower operator in the Dispatch Booth who was making sure everyone was properly loaded and seated. The underwater conveyor belt immediately pulled the two boats forward and dropped them in the dark waters of the bayou. The water currents took over and slowly pushed the boats past the Blue Bayou Restaurant on the right and the house-boats and alligator on the left. When Peter looked back to wave another thank you to Beth, his arm froze.

The security guard was standing on the un-loading dock looking right at him.

"I need you to stop the ride," he demanded to Beth.

"Whatever for?"

Pointing at the retreating boat, Todd told her, "I need that kid in the back row. I...I...uh, have his backpack," he finished lamely, holding up the item for her to see.

"That's not a reason to shut down an entire ride," Beth exclaimed, folding her arms over her chest and frowning at him. "If you want to leave the pack, I'll see that the boy gets it when he comes back around. The ride does exit right here, you know."

Todd turned his gaze from the boat that had almost reached the ride's interior. It was too late now. Even if he had jumped in the next boat, Peter would have a head start on him once they got back to the dock. Giving this ride operator the backpack was not an option. "I know the ride exits here," he snapped at the smart-aleck brunette. Seeing the other cast members start-ing to eye him suspiciously, he bit back his next retort. "I'll just wait and see that he gets it my-self, if that's okay with you," the sarcasm dripping off his words.

Beth couldn't see why this weird security guard was so interested in Peter and his backpack. She purposely left out the fact that she had known the boy since his birth. Having to get back to work, she saw the guard check his watch and back up a bit, finally out of everyone's way.

She knew she had about ten minutes before Peter would be back. And she wasn't going to let that guard touch even a hair on that boy's head.

As the boat entered the darkened interior of the ride, Peter could hear the screams of riders going down the first waterfall. He was relieved to see that the security guard hadn't boarded the next boat. Knowing at some point in the ride, boats usually catch up with each other, it was *possible* the guard could jump into his boat and take him captive again.

As Peter's boat hesitated under the talking skull warning him of the dangers that be ahead, his mind quickly went through some options. He had no doubt Todd would be waiting for him. He also had no doubt Aunt Beth would raise an uproar if he, Peter, indicated anything was wrong. As the launch plummeted down the first incline, he knew he didn't want to drag Aunt Beth into this just yet. There would be too many questions that he wasn't ready to answer. As he splashed down the second, easier slope, he knew what he had to do. There was one thing he was positive about—he could not return to the unloading dock.

That left only one option: He had to get off the ride before it got back to the dock.

And this was *not* an option that was approved of by the Park.

Knowing the ride as well as he did, he knew there were two good places to get off. The second best was before you rode up the waterfall at the end of the ride, just before the gunfight scene in the dynamite room. He knew the exit was behind the 'burning timbers' on the left. But, as he sat up straighter, the first—and best—choice was rapidly approaching. It was a soft blue tunnel on the left just across from Crab Island. He had only seconds to make his decision.

Scooting over to the left edge of his seat and glancing back to see that the following boat was far enough back that he wouldn't be seen, Peter waited until the boat drifted right next to the stone-like floor. As the other passengers in the boat were looking at the skeletons run through by swords, he quietly stood and as evenly as possible stepped onto the walkway. As soon as his feet hit the solid ground and no one had seen him, he ran for the tunnel and vanished behind the first bend.

Standing with his back firmly against the rock wall, he willed his breathing to return to normal and his heart to stop pounding loud enough for the next boat to hear him. As he calmed down, he looked to his right. There was a large tunnel that led directly into the Captain's Quarters. It was partially blocked by a large sea chest, but he could see the lower part of the ornate bed and its grisly occupant. He was so tempted to sneak over and see what was on the map that the skeleton Captain had been examining for decades with that magnifying glass!

With a silent laugh and a "what good would that do?" he turned to the deeper part of the tunnel and the exit door he knew was just beyond. Walking down the silent, bright white corridor, he wondered what he would have to say to Aunt Beth later that day. For surely she would notice his boat would come back without him. Exiting into a small walkway between New Orleans Square and Adventureland, Peter ignored the stares of guests who were curious about a non-costumed young man coming out of a cast-member-only door. Always interested in knowing what exciting things went on behind the scenes, some of the guests tried to look into the doorway before the door clicked shut. Something his dad had once told him floated through Peter's mind: "Always act like you know what you're doing and people will believe you."

Putting a small smile on his face, he calmly excused himself and walked through the line of people waiting for their turn to sail into the land of the pirates, knowing they all would get further through the ride than he had.

Catie, too, knew their game well, but didn't have any way to communicate once she and Peter ran their separate ways from the court-yard. For her, the closest ride was either the steam train or the Haunted Mansion. Since the train didn't offer any hiding place or protection, she chose the Mansion. Riding through the attraction as she was supposed to, she barely noticed the spooky effects. Once it was over, she walked to the exit and stood off to the side while the other riders departed through the crypt-like exit with echoes of a ghostly invitation to 'Hurry back' following them. Peeking around the corner, she was overcome with relief to see Peter waiting for her, though he too was out of the main flow of people. Not being able to stop herself, she ran into his arms. "I was so scared for you! I wanted to help but I didn't know what to do," she whispered into his chest as her arms encircled him. "Are you all right? Is he gone?"

Eyes closed for the moment, enjoying the knowledge that he wasn't alone in this, Peter allowed the hug for a couple of moments. Then, noticing the isn't-that-cute smiles on the faces of people walking around them, he suddenly became self-conscious and embarrassed. Pulling away from the tight grasp she had on him, he mumbled, "I'm okay, but my head hurts a little. He kept slamming me against the wall and it hurt!"

"I know," she said in a small voice, touching his arm with her fingertips. "I didn't know how to help. Since he was Security, I didn't know if I should yell for help or not."

Peter just nodded as he rubbed the sore spot on the back of his head. "I didn't know, either. I didn't recognize that guy. Don't know if he's new or he's somebody who somehow stole a uniform."

"Does that happen much?" the girl gasped, her eyes wide.

Peter gave a short shake of his head as he led her away from the congested exit of the Haunted Mansion. Going to the water's edge, they followed the black iron fence around the River. "Not with Wolf around it doesn't," he muttered. "I'll bet Wolf knows who this guy is."

"Should we tell him?"

Stopping right after the rafts over to Tom Sawyer Island, the two kids stood at the rail, watching a full canoe go by. It was near the end of the journey around Tom Sawyer Island and not too many of the guests were still paddling. Under different circumstances Peter would have suggested they go ride the canoes next. "No, I don't think we should yet. I'm not really hurt, and he just has my backpack. My favorite backpack," he muttered to himself, thinking. There was still some undone homework in there that will be a little hard to explain now. Peter turned to Catie and gave her a sudden smile. "But, he didn't get everything."

"What do you mean?" she asked, taken back by the grin. She didn't see much to smile about right then. Peter had gotten hurt. She had been threatened. Peter's backpack with the next clue was stolen. And they couldn't tell anyone. No, she couldn't see any reason why Peter would be smiling at her.

Peter held up his left hand, his palm facing her. "He didn't get everything," he cryptically told her.

Trying to look around his hand, she

frowned. "I don't get it."

Putting his hand back in front of her face, he explained, "I wrote it down twice. Once on the paper he probably has by now. And, here, on my hand!"

Eyes widening in recognition, Catie rewarded him with a dazzling smile so like her mother's. "Oh, Peter, you are so smart! What does it say?"

The look of pride dimmed a little. "I don't know," he admitted, looking at the scribble on his palm. "But, we will find out. And, I think I saw something while the guard was holding me." He pointed at the last word. "See that? Anges or something like that? I saw that word on a sign where we were near that blue staircase. It might mean something!"

Catie looked like she wanted to hug him again so he took a retreating step back, almost tripping on a baby stroller parked near the water's edge. "Oh, Peter, that is so exciting!" Her face fell again. "But, does that security guard have the same message, too?"

"Yeah, he does.... Wait a minute," his expressive face lit up again. "No, he doesn't! I hadn't written down all of the last word yet when I got drug out from under the piano thing. He only has a partial clue! We, on the other hand, have the whole thing." He looked at his hand and tried to pronounce, "**Cour d'Anges**," and failing miserably. "No problem. We'll figure it out."

Catie glanced at her watch. "Oh, we're late meeting Dad! We need to get going. He and

Alex are probably at the Pizza Port waiting for us. And I'm starved!"

As they hurried through Frontierland toward the Main Street hub, Catie timidly said, "Petey? This is still just between you and me, right?"

Allowing her to call him Petey just this one time, he smiled as they went past the Partners Statue of Walt and Mickey surrounded by white and purple tulips. "Yeah, just you and me. We'll see where this clue takes us together." *And I'll tell you about your mom later*, he promised to himself. *Or, she will, more than likely.*

Catie gave a small sigh as they quick-walked between the spinning Astro Orbitors and Star Tours, heading to the far corner of Tomor-rowland and the popular Pizza Port restaurant. They could see the tall white and red Moonliner rocket next to the entrance and kept their eyes on that as they walked, each deep in their own thoughts.

After waiting an extra ten minutes, and watching countless boatloads of guests stream-ing past him, Todd knew he had been out-smarted by that brat. And that stupid brunette on duty didn't even seem to notice that the kid never came back.

About to utter something foul, he raised his hands in frustration. Only his right hand was weighted down. With Peter's backpack.

The angry look of defeat was replaced with one of glee. "I have the clue!" he muttered to himself. Without a backwards glance, he left the unloading dock and ducked back into the relative quiet of the courtyard. Todd turned his attention to the blue and red pack and pulled open every pocket. Rifling through the contents, he finally came to the scrap of paper with three words hastily written: Cour d' A. With a shout of victory, he was about to cast aside the backpack when he remembered the listening bug he had planted in there that fateful day in the Tiki Room.

Pulling out the small silver disc, he gave it a lighthearted kiss and dropped it in his pocket. Sauntering back out onto the main walkway of New Orleans Square and looking around to see that no one was watching, he unceremoniously dumped the backpack into the nearest trashcan. Glancing at his watch he saw that he would be off duty in ten minutes. Secure in knowing the kids wouldn't tell anyone what had happened without giving away their own deceit, he slowly walked back to his patrol in Fantasyland to finish his shift.

Once the weird guard had left the dock, Beth immediately went to the phone hidden in the ride's secondary control podium and punched in Security's number. Asking to be transferred to Wolf, she waited anxiously. Peter's not coming back was big. Something had to have happened with that security guard to make him jump ship. She now knew that was exactly what Peter had done. With a secret smile she admitted to herself that she knew exactly *where* he had jumped, too.

Her pleasant memories were interrupted when Wolf came on the line. In a hushed voice she ran down all the facts she had about the guard named Todd and the missing Peter. She wasn't surprised when he told her he would take care of it and not to worry. Peter would be safe, he had added.

Knowing Adam and Alex were somewhere in the Park, Beth contemplated calling them on her cell phone. She held back, trusting Wolf. But, she would expect explanations from Peter and Catie when she got home, make no mistake about that!

On patrol duty in Critter Country, Wolf put away his walkie-talkie. A concerned frown lined his features. He now had a face to go with the mysterious man who had helped Peter and Michael in the Tiki Room—and he didn't like it.

It was one of his own security guards, one that he had never really liked for some unknown reason.

He headed over toward Fantasyland where he knew Raven was assigned. Through some covert observation, maybe Wolf could learn something about the man.

Arriving there, he soon learned that Todd Raven was already off duty.

CHAPTER 10

"Hey, Lance, when are those steaks going to be done?" Mark called over to him from the middle of the pool.

"Steaks? Who said you leeches get steak?" Lance threw back at him, not even looking up as he was busily flipping burgers, hot dogs, and T-bones on his huge stainless steel grill. "These babies are mine."

The cascade of water Mark aimed at his security buddy fell way short of its intended goal. Laughing and unfazed by the jibe, Mark turned his pool float back around to his companion.

Emerging from the back of the house, Kimberly walked down the grassy slope of their backyard bearing a large pitcher of iced tea and came to a sudden halt. Looking around, she saw she was fairly surrounded by a huge amount of thirsty guests. Not knowing where to start, she gamely shrugged and headed for the two Peoplemover cars they had set up as a picnic area. Four couples were talking and laughing as they sat under the white fiberglass roof of the cars. "Great party, Kimberly," one of the Park's princesses told her, holding out a plastic tumbler for a refill. "As always! Your yard looks great. How did you ever find those Skyway cabins over there? I never would have imagined them used as gazebos. Great idea."

Looking over at the gently swinging pale blue and yellow gondolas hanging under their own wooden frames, Kimberly gave a fond smile. She had always loved the Skyway ride that had gone from Fantasyland through the Matterhorn, and then dropped down into the Tomorrowland station. Opening in 1956, it had a long run until it was shut down in 1994. Shaking her head as if she couldn't believe it herself, she answered, "Thanks, Amber. We heard about this auction over in Buena Park and thought we'd check it out. And there they were, sitting on the ground, tilted over like they were falling apart. We couldn't resist."

"Wow, I didn't know any of them were still out there. What else did you find?" asked the petite brunette, intrigued now. Even without the black wig of her costume, it was easy to see her portraying Snow White.

Giving her a saucy wink, Kimberly—who had portrayed both Belle and Cinderella—sauntered off. "Oh, you'll just have to go exploring and find out!"

A shout from the grassy expanse at the west end of the yard got everyone's attention. After watching for a moment, Kimberly turned back and handed the already-empty pitcher to one of the high-school students they had hired to help serve everyone. "Thanks, Joey," she said. Indicating the commotion with her chin, she added with a laugh, "I'm going to go check that out. Come on over yourself when your hour shift is over."

"Will do, Mrs. B.," Joey replied, heading back to the kitchen for a refill.

As Kimberly got closer to the noise, a broad smile broke out on her face. Kicking off her sandals, she grabbed up a racquet that had been thrown onto the grass and jumped into the fray. It appeared to be some form of Tag Team Badminton with at least eight people on each side of the court, two shuttlecocks, one tennis ball, and an occasional Frisbee. Two of the security guards playing were wearing football helmets and had a colorful strip of cloth hanging from their back pocket.

"We get Kimberly!" someone buried in the mass of people shouted from the other side of the net.

Ducking under the volleyball net, Kimberly gamely asked, "Okay, what do I do?"

"Whatever you want! Fore!"

Ten racquets started swinging madly at the just-launched tennis ball. Once the ball made it over the net, two women rushed in from the sidelines and tagged out two others. The two who were tagged went under the net and joined the other side.

"Traitors!"

"Sore losers!"

"Losers? Who's losing? What's the score?"

"I thought you were keeping score."

"Fore!"

"Heads up!"

The volleyball game going on over on the other side of the yard wasn't much more organized. Stuck with the smaller badminton net that was being held higher in the air by two of the guards, the teams were making do. One side had approximately eleven players and the opponents had anywhere from eight to fourteen depending on who was hungry or who decided to go swimming between serves. The two-hit rule per side seemed to be out the window as the ball got at least four assists to get over the net and the yell of "Do over!" was met with good-natured compliance. The guards holding up the net seemed to be playing for both sides and tried to keep the ball from going out of bounds by running the net over to wherever it was needed.

Alex and Catie's dad Adam wandered over to the barbecue grill, soda in his hands. Lance noticed he was limping slightly.

"What happened? Beth get mad and kick you in the shin?"

"Almost," he said with a grimace. "I thought I'd try a round of croquet."

Lance let out a sympathy whistle. "Ooh, that's too bad. How big is the court this time?"

Adam had to think. "Well, it starts in the front yard—your front yard this year," he clarified with a grin, "goes through the garage, down the slope around the badminton arena, across the pond somehow—never did figure the angle on that wicket—and into the neighbor's yard two houses over. Good thing they aren't home," he muttered, taking a sip of his soda.

Lance looked disappointed. "Wow, they really shortened the course this year. How many are playing?"

"Fifteen to thirty. Hope you weren't too attached to those golf clubs we found in the garage. We were a little short of mallets."

Chuckling, Lance sliced a hunk off of one of the steaks and handed it to Adam. "This done yet?"

Adam gave him an amused look. "Since when don't you know how to barbecue?" Popping it in his mouth, Adam closed his eyes and sighed. "Oh, man, that's tender! I'll take that one."

Plopping the steak on a plate, Lance opened a small door on the lower half of the grill. "Baked potato or fries?"

"Yes."

"Corn on the cob?"

Adam stuck a fry in his mouth and his eyes suddenly widened. A horde of swimmers saw his steak and began advancing on the grill. "I'll eat quick and then take over the grill so you can have some fun," Adam called back over his shoulder as he hurried away from the barbecue just in time to avoid being trampled.

Using his barbeque fork as a weapon, Lance tried to defend his grill, but was outnumbered. Calling over the dripping heads surrounding him, he told Adam, "Thanks. What's left of me will be waiting for you to get back! Back, back you moochers!" he yelled, waving the long fork like a sword at the sea of plates being held out to him.

With a grin, Adam headed for the umbrella tables set up in a relatively quiet corner of the yard. Beth soon joined him with her own plate, looking back at the melee at the grill. "Wow, don't security guards ever eat at home?" she laughed. "I don't know if Lance will survive."

"It's not just the security guards. Some of those princesses can get pretty feisty. Hey, how did you get your food so fast? I didn't see you at the grill," he eyed her plate suspiciously. Her steak looked like a filet mignon—definitely not a T-bone.

"I know the chef."

Adam wasn't convinced. "Everyone here knows the chef. Is that a filet? Where were those? I never saw any potato salad."

Beth closed her eyes in bliss as she took her first bite of steak. "I'm not telling. Haven't you been inside the house?"

Adam was finishing off his fries and was considering grabbing her hot garlic French bread. "No, not since we got here. Why? What's inside?"

"Check out the kitchen," was all she said as she took a huge bite out of the bread, and then held it away from him. "Hands off, Adam," she warned him with a grin.

"Bet you hear that a lot," Lance kidded Adam when he suddenly appeared at their table and sat in one of the empty chairs, putting his high-piled plate on the table.

Surprised, Adam looked over at the grill still

surrounded by a mass of people. "How did you get out of that mess? And with food?"

"Wolf took over," was all Lance had to say.

"Ah," Adam and Beth said together as they bent back to finish their meal.

"Yeah," Lance nodded. "Now the kids might have a chance to eat!" he laughed.

Finished with her food, much to the dismay of her husband, Beth pushed her wicker chair back and looked over the huge backyard. "Are there more here than last year?"

Lance shrugged, biting into his own filet.

"How come I didn't get a filet?" Adam wanted to know, wondering if he should go check out the kitchen.

Ignoring him, Lance answered Beth's question. "I think so. It's pretty much an open invitation for the Security Department and the princess people and whoever they want to bring along. They come and go as their schedules allow. Hold on," he got up as the abused volleyball somehow made it all the way across the yard. They could faintly hear 'a little help, please!' With a heave, Lance sent the ball into the pool, barely missing some kids playing Marco Polo by the waterfall. "Oops. Anyway, some will be back after their shift is over," he resumed as he sat back in his chair. "I was surprised Wolf got here so early. He usually shows up around ten at night when it's sort of winding down. Glad to see him, though."

"Well, Alex and Catie are having a great time," Beth told him, looking around. "At least I think they are. I haven't actually seen them since we got here."

"Oh, they're fine," Lance waved her off with his fork as he finished the last of his food. "I think Michael is guarding Dug with his life. They're probably all together. Somewhere…," he trailed off, unconcerned as he stretched out his long legs and appeared to want to take a nap.

Lance might not have known exactly where all the kids were at that moment, but someone else did. Todd Raven was among the happy revelers at the Brentwood home. After striking out with the newest Aurora and getting slapped in the face by Mulan, he had filled his plate at the barbecue, idly wondering why Wolf seemed to stare right through him to his soul. Seated by himself near the house, he carefully watched all that was going on as he ate.

He was paying close attention when Kimberly finally went to join her husband at the far side of the lawn. When the horde of kids went screaming around to the front of the house, he saw the chance he had been waiting for.

Getting slowly to his feet, he made a show of stretching out his arms as if he was very content and a little sleepy. Saying, "Bathroom," to no one in particular, he wandered in through the back door after making sure Wolf was busy at the grill and didn't see him. Grabbing an éclair off a silver serving tray, he popped it in his mouth as he went through the massive, busy kitchen. Seeing that nobody was paying him any attention, he took his time in walking down the hallway as if looking for the bathroom for guests that was actually just off the kitchen. He nodded a greeting to a couple just leaving the living room where they had been checking out the Mr. Toad's ride car in the corner. Using that as a pretense, Todd ambled over to the red and black car. Running a hand along the tufted black leather seat, he glanced over his shoulder. There was no one around.

Taking advantage of the moment, he bounded up the stairs, his heart pounding. He knew the yard was filled with security guards—and Wolf—so he knew he had to make it quick. Glancing into the open doors of the many bedrooms, he finally found the one that he thought would be Peter's. It was the posters on the walls and the lack of toys that made him sure this was the correct room.

He didn't dare close the door as none of the doors in the long hallway had been closed. Quickly going to the bed where he knew Peter had stashed the items from the capsules, he thrust his right arm under the mattress. "That bug was worth every penny," he muttered quietly to himself, his hand finally coming in contact with something solid.

Pulling the object out, Todd was dismayed it wasn't one of the keys Peter had said he had found. This looked like it was some piece of exercise equipment. Trying again, Todd shoved the hand grip back and felt around again. This time he felt the edge of something made of paper and his heart rate sped up again. "Finally," he grumbled.

Todd stared at the clue that he was sure was written in Walt's own handwriting. "This has to be worth a fortune," as he greedily stuffed it into his pocket. After another fruitless search under the mattress and a quick look through the desk drawers, it was obvious Peter had found a new hiding place for the animation cel and, more importantly, the keys he needed. "What? Doesn't the brat trust anybody?" he wondered as he peeked down the hallway.

About ready to steal downstairs, Todd spotted a door he had missed the first time. This door was closed. *Unusual,* he thought. *Why is that one closed? Yet another bathroom maybe?*

Trying to open the door quietly, hoping it didn't have squeaky hinges, he was astonished to find it was not a room at all. It was an elevator.

"Why the heck would they have an elevator? Too lazy to use the stairs?"

Stepping inside, he closed the door for more privacy in examining it. "Third floor? For real? Sheesh, must be nice," he groused as he pushed the number three. Immediately the elevator started rising. "Well, might as well check it out while I'm here."

As the lift came to a stop, he opened the door and found himself in an obviously little-used part of the house. Stepping out, he glanced around at the stacks of cardboard boxes and cast-off furniture and paintings. "Buncha junk," Todd muttered, holding back from running a finger through the dust, knowing better than to leave any tell-tale fingerprints behind. But he also knew enough to look for something he might be able to pawn later. Some of the larger boxes were marked Disney Memorabilia.

His attention was diverted again when he spotted a closed door on the other side of the elevator. Missing it when he saw all the boxes, he turned back and tried the doorknob, using a handkerchief over his fingers.

"Now why would they lock a door in the attic?" he mumbled to himself, his hand on his chin as he thought. Carefully examining the wall on each side of the door, his eyes narrowed. "Oh ho, what's this?"

Again using the handkerchief, he lifted a small panel that he had just spotted next to the door frame. Carefully covered with the same old-fashioned flocked wallpaper as the rest of the room, it was almost completely invisible to the casual eye. The small panel hid a numerical keypad. "Curiouser and curiouser," as he stepped back and used his trained thief's eye to take stock. "It's dusty over in that part of the room, but it's clean on this side of the elevator. The brass doorknob on my mystery door is dust free and obviously well used. The wear and tear of the carpet shows this door is the only path after exiting the elevator, and the carpet is very worn, showing years of use. Behind this door must be something of considerable value," he concluded. "And, I'll never have a better chance to see what it is."

Being a successful thief meant he had learned to never just jump into something. Cautious, he first went to the stairway that also came up to this floor, and carefully listened for any sign of life on the second floor below him. When he was finally satisfied that he would not be interrupted, he turned back to the keypad and smiled in anticipation.

"Peter, you never showed me the Gold Pass thing you said you found at the Studio," Catie was saying as they sat in the shade. They were tired out after playing a marathon game of croquet.

"Want to see it now?" he asked, watching Michael carry Dug over to some bushes. "He really needs to let that dog walk now and then," he muttered.

"Sure. Do you want to bring it here, or is it okay if I go up to your room?" she asked, letting him decide the boundaries.

"I'll get it. My room's a mess. Be right back," he promised, springing to his feet.

Once in his room, he felt under his mattress for the Gold Pass and the clue. Confused when he couldn't find the papers, he then noticed that his hidden hand grip was too near the edge. "Has Michael been in my stuff?" he wondered, pushing up the bulky mattress as best he could to find the missing items. "No, he wouldn't do that. He wasn't that interested in the quest."

When he exonerated his brother, he had to then wonder who did take the Pass—because it was definitely missing. It worried him because he now knew the value of it and how it would admit him into any Disney Park around the world. Letting the mattress fall back into place with a dusty *Whoosh*, he puts his hands on his hips and looked around his room with narrowed, suspicious eyes. His desk looked messy, but, then, it always did. However, he knew his pile of school books hadn't been strewn over the desk like that.

"Somebody's been in my room," he concluded, his eyes getting wide. Just as he was about to go downstairs to get his dad, he noticed the door to the elevator. He had been banned from using it since he was five and had spent hours playing in it, riding up and down. But that didn't mean he didn't notice things. Only members of the family knew about the red flag that popped over the latch indicating the door was locked and that the elevator was on a different floor. Always left on the second floor, Peter knew someone had recently used the lift. Up or down?

Peter glanced at the stairs and decided to first go upstairs to check it out. He had been banned from the attic, too, after a rambunctious game of pirates on the antique sofas placed there for safekeeping. Treading softly on the heavily carpeted stairs, his mouth dried out as he neared the landing and his heart starting beating heavily. Reminding himself that if there *was* anyone there, it was probably just a nosy guest from the party. Licking his dry lips, he cautiously peeked around the corner when his eyes became level with the floor.

Seeing no one, he gave a surprised,

"Hmm", and climbed one more step. Always curious about the places he wasn't allowed, he forgot all about Catie waiting for him and his missing items as he decided to explore a little. "I'm already here," he reasoned with a half-grin. Hand on the rail, he was about to head for the stack of Disney boxes when he stopped dead in his tracks. The door to the secret room he had never been allowed to enter was slightly ajar. Mouth open in surprise, Peter climbed the last step and just stood there. Not only had he never been inside, he had never actually even seen the door open, let alone his mom or dad going in or out. The room was never even talked about. And now it was open! Whichever parent was in there, he quickly decided he would simply say he heard a noise and wanted to make sure everything was all right. *Yeah, that will work*, he told himself as he boldly entered the room, excited about whatever he was finally going to get to see.

Thinking about it later, Peter couldn't have said what surprised him more—seeing the contents of the room or seeing the security guard who had held him captive going through the file cabinets in that room.

Likewise surprised was Todd Raven. Hearing a startled gasp behind him, in one smooth motion, Todd pulled a switchblade out of his pocket and swirled around. The blade was pointed at the intruder and steady in his hand.

"You!" they each said in unison.

"Don't!" Todd warned as Peter made a move to leap from the room. "Get in here," he yelled, motioning with the knife and indicating a chair. "Sit down right there and don't move again!"

Seeing the knife wasn't wavering to indicate fear or indecision, Peter reluctantly did as he was told. "How come I never saw you at the party?" he demanded, trying not to sound frightened.

"I made sure you didn't," Todd snapped at him. "As I guessed correctly, you did recognize me. Couldn't have you running to that meddler Wolf, now could I?" he asked, distracted as he held the knife toward Peter with one hand and pulled something out of the filing cabinet with the other.

Knowing he wasn't expected to answer, Peter's wide, angry eyes went back and forth from the sharp blade in front of him to the holographic map in the center of the room.

Seeing Peter eyeing the map, Todd turned back to him as he stuffed some more papers into his pocket. "What is this place? Explain. And while you are at it, I want that last clue. Tell me where it is in here. Now!" as he held the blade closer to the boy's throat without actually touching him.

Peter tried to swallow, but his mouth was dry. "I...I don't know what this room is. I've never been in here before," he answered about this strange, intriguing room, quickly deciding to say nothing about the clue.

Looking around at al the monitors and ter-

minals, Todd didn't seem to remember his de-
mand for the last clue. He was still trying to figure out all the complex machinery in the room.
"Liar! You have one minute to explain
this…this…whatever this room is."

"I…don't…know," stated Peter. "I've never
seen this stuff before."

Not liking his answer but realizing the boy
was probably telling the truth, he grabbed Peter
out of the chair. Dragging him across the room,
Peter was shoved next to a different filing cabinet that Todd wanted to check out before he left.
"Do not move and do not try me," he warned in
his sternest voice.

Nodding mutely, Peter let his eyes take in
the monitors that were showing various places
obviously within Disneyland. Some of the cameras must have been set in dark rooms somewhere because only vague outlines of items
could be seen.

"What's going on here?!"

"Mom! He's got a knife. Run!"

"Peter!" she yelled as Todd swung around
and grabbed the boy's shoulders, pulling him
close, the knife under his chin.

"Get in here, Kimberly," the man holding her
son ordered, motioning with the wicked-looking
knife.

At first curious as to why someone had
used the elevator and wondering what they were
doing, Kimberly was overcome by the surprise
of finding anyone in the supposedly locked War
Room—and that it was a party guest holding her
son hostage. Her mind spinning, Kimberly

silently realized her best option right then was to do as she was told.

"Over there, away from the door," Todd demanded, pointing at the chair he had used for Peter earlier. "Sit while I think. It's getting way too crowded in here."

As Kimberly purposely sank into a different chair at the main control desk, her hand quickly went to a button hidden under the desktop. Her eyes never dropping from the man holding her son, she smoothly brought her hand back to her lap, silently hoping either Lance or Wolf—or both—were wearing their pagers that day. As her wide eyes continued to stare at Peter and the knife aimed at him, she unconsciously rubbed the knife scars on her own arms. She, too, had been held at knifepoint. Glancing at the desktop next to her, there were plenty of heavy items she could use as a weapon, but she was too far away. She'd never make it over to the security guard without being seen. Nor could she take a chance throwing something because Peter was too close to the thief. Frustrated by her helplessness and knowing how scared Peter must be feeling, her ears desperately listened for any sound indicating Wolf or Lance might be outside the door.

Always prepared for a possible heist and any contingency, Todd pulled a plastic zip tie out of his pants pocket. Next to it had been the listening bug he had forgotten to drop in Peter's room, a piece of duct tape, and a well-used set of lock picks. Shoving Peter forward, he gave him the zip tie. "Pull her hands behind the chair and fasten them together with this. I've got to get out of here and I can't take both of you with me. She'd be too much to handle downstairs. And, if you don't pull it tight? I'll start by cutting off one finger," he threatened.

"Sorry, Mom," Peter whispered miserably as he complied with the demands of his captor.

"It will be all right, honey," she whispered back. "What are you going to do with him?" Kimberly demanded out loud, her green eyes flashing as she held her two hands slightly apart behind her so she would have some movement after Peter was through.

"If you don't shut up, I'm going to use the duct tape I brought," warned the thief, his bravado only a show as his heart was beating so hard he thought it was going to burst. He hadn't expected to be discovered. *This is why I hate breaking and entering*, he reminded himself sourly. "I'm going to take the boy somewhere 'safe' and then you and I are going to have a nice, long talk about this room after all your *guests* are gone," he spat at Kimberly whose eyes opened even wider at his words.

"No, don't take him! He's only a boy. I'll…I'll go with you and tell you whatever you want. Just leave him here," she pleaded.

"Oh, you'll tell me all right, but he's my safety out of here right now. He may be only a boy, as you say, but he's been involved in some pretty serious stuff I'll bet *you* don't even know about." Bringing a piece of paper out of his pocket, Todd held up the Gold Pass for her to see. "Like this, for instance."

"Hey, that's mine," an angry Peter shouted as he grabbed at the Pass.

Todd raised his arm to cuff him with the hilt of the knife, but held back. "Do that again and she'll lose an ear."

"Where did you get that?" demanded Kimberly, immediately recognizing what he was holding. Not even realizing what she was doing, her eyes went over to one of the filing cabinets.

"Oh, I didn't get it there," Todd told her with a smirk. "Your little darling here dug it up at the Studio, didn't you, Petey? I got plenty out of that file, though. We'll have a lot to talk about later," promised the thief as he prodded Peter in the ribs with the tip of the knife. "Out the door and down the stairs. One peep and I push this into your spine. Got it?"

Peter had no option but to comply. He nodded silently and gave his mom one last, miserable look. He could see tears running down her cheek and his heart clenched.

Todd closed the door behind them, hoping the room was soundproof. He had a feeling Kimberly would start yelling her head off as soon as he was down the stairs. Putting the knife out of sight in his pocket, he still held it against the boy's back as his other hand held tightly onto Peter's arm. "No tricks," he warned again when they got to the first floor and headed for the front door. Always planning ahead for any possibility, he had parked a ways down the street so he would be able to leave in a hurry if he needed to. He now found that it had been a good plan since many of the cars were hemmed in all over the curved driveway and into the street.

Relaxing a little with every step away from the house, Todd still kept a grip on the boy's arm. But now he was more hopeful that they wouldn't be discovered before they could get away. It was doubtful anyone would find Kimberly soon. And, if they did, they would have to get Lance to open the combination. He also doubted it would be done openly given the odd contents of that room. Yes, he figured he had plenty of time and wouldn't need to call attention to himself by speeding.

Parked on the other side of the street, facing the wrong direction, Todd was just about to open the passenger door of his car to shove Peter inside. Across from where they had just crossed the wide street, Wolf suddenly stepped out from behind a tree. Eyes blazing with hatred, the dark security guard stared at him as if willing him to die where he stood.

"Let the boy go."

The words were spoken softly, almost too soft to hear in the distance that separated them. But the force of the words hit Todd directly in the chest. The intensity was as strong as a physical blow.

"Let the boy go," he repeated louder, taking two steps closer to Todd's car.

Eyes wide, Todd didn't see any weapon in Wolf's hand. As a matter of fact, those fisted hands in question were being held out slightly away from his body as if showing Todd he was unarmed. "I don't think I'm going to obey your command this time," the shaken security guard said, trying to sound smooth and in charge, the knife back out in the open. "I get enough of that at work. Get in the car, boy."

"It's locked," Peter lied, hoping it would confuse Todd enough to give Wolf an advantage.

Not expecting any comment from the boy, let alone any hesitation or argument, his mouth fell open. "What?" Peter's idea worked as Todd appeared to be momentarily baffled.

Sensing his confusion, Wolf saw his chance. He yelled in Lakota, "Wana, kuta. Kagniya!" hoping the boy remembered his lessons. *Now, drop. Roll!*

Without question, Peter dropped like a brick and rolled away from his attacker.

Suddenly exposed, Todd turned erratically, not knowing exactly what to do.

Wolf's hand shot out like a streak of lightning. The rock he had concealed in his fist smashed through the passenger window, missing Todd by less than an inch.

Seeing Wolf starting to move toward him and knowing his hostage was now out of his reach, Todd hurled himself over the hood of his car and jumped into the driver's seat. Jamming the key into the ignition just as Wolf got to the passenger side of the car and was reaching in through the broken window, he started the engine and slammed the car into drive.

Wolf had to jump back or his arm would have been ripped open by the broken glass. He bit back a curse as the car sped down the street, narrowly missing several parked cars as it vanished around the corner.

"I hope he misses the sharp curve and hur-tles off the edge of the mountain," Peter spat out when he ran over next to his deliverer.

"Mis eya." *Me, too.* Still under the effects of adrenaline and hatred, Wolf forgot to switch back to English.

"How did you know?" asked Peter when they finally turned to go back to the house. "Is Mom all right?"

"She hit the panic button in the…the, uh, of-fice," he frowned, not knowing, at this point, how much the boy knew. "I was just coming in when I saw Raven take you out the front door."

Peter smiled up at him. "You missed," refer-ring to the rock Wolf had thrown at Todd.

"Hmm, I know. Never happened before. Let's not tell your dad."

Peter suddenly stopped walking. It took a couple of steps before Wolf realized the boy wasn't beside him. "Uncle Wolf?" he looked up at his friend with watery eyes, but he wouldn't let himself cry. "Philámayaye." *Thank you.*

Wolf put a comforting arm around Peter's narrow shoulders and held him tight. "You're welcome. I'm glad you're all right. Your mom was so mad she was spitting nails."

"There's some things I've been doing that you don't know about," Peter slowly told him. "I found something Walt Disney left behind and this Todd guy somehow found out about it. He…he stole one of my clues."

Wolf hesitated for a long minute before an-swering. It really wasn't his place. It was up to Lance and Kimberly to tell the boy about the

Guardians and the clues. But, Todd was on his security force. "I know," the warrior admitted. "I actually know everything you found. But, we will have to talk about that later. Let me ask you this, though. Did Raven get the keys?"

A look of shock passed quickly over Peter's open face. Uncle Wolf never ceased to amaze him. Of course Uncle Wolf knew. All the questions tumbling through Peter's mind would have to wait. "No," was his answer. "Well, I don't think so. I got kinda nervous about them because I *think* they are really important, so I moved them to a new hiding place a couple of nights ago." Stopping for a moment, he added, "I didn't check, though. Should we go look to see if they are still there? Yeah, probably," Peter answered himself and fell silent again. "Do you know where they fit?"

"Yes. But that's for you to figure out."

Peter gave a deep sigh. "I was afraid you would say that."

Giving the boy a friendly slap on his shoulder as they walked up the driveway, dodging a red croquet ball that went skidding past them, Wolf quietly said, "We'd better go tell your mom you're okay. She must be frantic by now."

"Then are you going after Todd?" was the hopeful question, the light of revenge shining in the green eyes staring at him.

Wolf gave a low growl deep in his chest. "No, much as I'd like to. But, I do know where he will go next."

"Where's that?"

"The same place you will be."

"That ought to be fun," the boy mumbled as his mom and dad came running from the house, relief plastered over their faces.

Wolf gave a slight smile. He wasn't sure which thing the boy was referring to—his parents or the next encounter with Todd.

Either way, Wolf would be there—and the boy would be safe.

CHAPTER 11

Wolf was on guard at the door to Lance's study. When any of the unsuspecting partiers came looking for Lance or Kimberly they were simply told, "Go away." And, since it was Wolf, they did.

Once Kimberly and Lance realized Peter was not hurt and that Todd got away, the high emotions began to settle. Not wanting to alarm or alert any of the security force that something was amiss, the three family members, at Wolf's suggestion, retreated from prying eyes into the privacy of the study.

"Mom! Quit hovering! I'm fine, I promise!" Peter was exclaiming yet again. Even though he had been badly shaken, after his parents' long, heartfelt hug out on the driveway, he was done with the smothering.

Remembering he was thirteen and not five years old, the mom in Kimberly backed off and she sat on the other leather sofa. Her hands might not be able to touch him, but her eyes still examined every inch of her son that showed.

Seeing her look, Peter sighed. "Mom! I'm fine. He…he didn't cut me," his voice catching in spite of himself. He had been terrified. Clearing his throat, Peter repeated steadier, "He didn't hurt me. My arms are bruised, but that's all."

Seeing the red marks on his son's arm, Lance became furious again. "I'll…I'll find that dirty…and…I'll…." Lance paced the room, unable to put his anger into proper words. He ran a frustrated hand through his hair.

"Honey, please sit," Kimberly patted the sofa next to her with a little more force than was necessary. "I know how you feel. I could rip his arms out of his sockets and stuff them down his throat, but that doesn't help right now. We need to discuss this rationally."

Perched on the edge of his desk now, Lance crossed his arms in front of his chest. His ranting stopped, but his eyes still snapped in fury. "I know. You're right," he replied in a calmer voice, looking out the window but not seeing any of the partying that was still going on in full swing. They had decided to let everyone continue to enjoy themselves outside, not dragging anyone in on their private matter. "But I can't just do nothing. How did he know about the…the room upstairs, Wolf?"

After a quick glance into the hallway, Wolf didn't see anyone else likely to interrupt them. Clicking the door shut, he turned to the three pairs of eyes staring at him. "I don't know," he admitted. He looked at Peter, gauging his readiness for disclosure. "Peter? Do you agree this is the time to talk?"

Nodding mutely, Peter stood. "I need to get a couple of things from my room. I'll be right back."

Even though the threat was no longer in their house, Kimberly hated to see him leave the safety of the room. She reached out a hand, but pulled it back and looked miserably at Lance. Understanding, he told her quietly, "Let him go."

Everyone but Wolf was surprised at the items Peter set out in front of them on the massive mahogany desktop. Wolf, relieved to see the two brass keys amongst the other items, hung back and just observed. His part would come later.

The anger forgotten for the moment, Lance held up the animation cel of Mickey Mouse. "This is in pristine condition! And signed by Walt!" His eyes fell on the yellow-edged notepaper that held the message from Walt and the individual clues. From his own past experiences, he immediately recognized them for what they were. With his fingertips resting on the edge of one of the clues, he asked Peter, "Why didn't you come to us when you found this letter?"

"Because you wouldn't understand."

"Wouldn't understand what, honey?" Kimberly asked in a soft voice even though her heart had sped up considerably once she saw the familiar notepaper.

"That this was something Michael and I needed to do together."

"Michael?" both parents repeated in shock, instantly looking at Wolf. "Michael is in this, too? Where is he!?"

Wolf held up a calming hand when it looked as if both Kimberly and Lance were going to rush out of the room to look for their other sons. "He's fine. He just carried that puppy past the window again. Don't know what he's going to do when the dog outweighs him...." Looking at Peter for an okay, the boy gave him a brief nod. "Michael was with Peter when they pulled this, the first letter, out of the Golden Horseshoe." At the confused looks that crossed the parents' faces, he added, "You were all there that day. It was Michael who inadvertently found the hiding place. He and Peter went back once they got you and Andrew to go elsewhere." Wolf gave a small smile as he thought back. "I remember when Walt knocked that hole in the wall. He was pretty mad. But, like Walt, he found a way to turn it to his advantage and made it one of his hiding places."

"You mean, like the Tiki Room and the Mutoscope thing," Peter asked, a little confused by Wolf's words. The way he was talking, Wolf made it sound much *bigger* somehow than what he knew about.

Seeing the curious look in the boy's eyes and not desiring to go there just yet, Wolf simply acknowledged, "Yeah, something like that."

Seeing that the story was in danger of getting sidetracked, Lance brought the discussion back around to Peter's discovery. "So after you found the letter, I take it you found something in the Tiki Room and a...what did you call it? Mute something?"

"Mutoscope, Dad. It's that machine in the Penny Arcade that plays an old-time movie when you turn the crank. This one was Charlie Chaplin and was about a baker...," he drifted off when he saw that his dad wasn't interested in the actual movie. "Anyway, when we put in enough pennies, the movie changed to one showing Walt in the Tiki room and pointing at a face on the side wall." He looked over at Wolf, a frown on his face. "That was the first time I saw that Todd guy. In the Tiki Room. He came over to help when the cast member caught us getting into the tiki. But, I didn't see him when we rode the Lilly Belle."

"That doesn't mean he wasn't there watching somehow," Wolf muttered.

Kimberly spoke up. "Wait a minute. The Lilly Belle was part of this? Is that why we rode it that day? I always wondered about that coming up all of a sudden." She glanced suspiciously at Wolf, her green eyes narrowed as she tried to figure it all out. The capsule in the Lilly Belle hadn't been indicated on the holographic map in the War Room, but she couldn't bring that up yet. "And you set it up. How long did you know what they were doing?"

Wolf gave her an unconcerned shrug. "I didn't figure it out until I saw Catie pull the capsule from one of the sofas and give it to Peter."

"Catie?" both parents echoed in surprise. "She's in on this, too?"

Peter slapped his forehead. "Catie! I forgot

about Catie. She's been waiting for me to show her the Gold Pass thing Todd stole."

"What Gold Pass?" Lance asked, moving aside the papers on his desk and not seeing one.

"Todd found it under…in my hiding place," Peter answered vaguely. "You know what a Gold Pass is?" He sounded somewhere between surprised and impressed.

Lance simply nodded and ignored the explanation Peter seemed to be expecting. He wasn't concerned about the Pass right now. Looking at Wolf, he wanted to know, "Should we bring in Adam and Beth? Is Catie in danger, too?"

Wolf slowly shook his head. "From what has happened, I think Raven is just concentrating on Peter right now." He caught the distressed look that came over Kimberly's face at his words. "He'll be fine, Kimberly. I'm sure of that."

Peter cleared his throat. And, just as suddenly as he did, all eyes in the room were turned expectedly to him. If he had been standing, he would have taken a step backwards. "Umm, Catie was with me when Todd grabbed us coming out of Club 33 the second time." When an angry look flooded his dad's face again, he hurriedly explained, "There was a clue on the bottom of the harpsichord and we had to get back in. I pretended to be you and the woman at the desk let us right in."

Lance ignored the smiling look Kimberly gave him. "What do you mean 'Todd grabbed us'? Literally or figuratively? I mean, did he really grab you?"

Peter nodded. "Yeah. Well, he dragged me by my backpack into the Court of Angels." He left out the part about his head being repeatedly banged against the wall. His dad was already mad enough. "He didn't touch Catie until he was about to take us backstage to hide us somewhere. That's when I shoved him and we got away. I went to Pirates where Aunt Beth was working and got on the ride right away. When I saw that Todd had followed *me*, I knew Catie was safe. I was afraid he would catch up to me on the ride, so I, uh, jumped off the ride," he mumbled, dropping his eyes as he fully expected to get in trouble for jumping out of the Pirate boat and going backstage.

"Yeah, right at the blue tunnel," Lance was saying, nodding as he thought it all over.

"How do you know that?" Peter wanted to know.

Lance's eyes turned back to the boy. "Oh, I just know the spot, that's all," as he gave his son a secret smile and turned back to Wolf before Peter could ask him any more about it. "Maybe we should go get Adam and Beth and let them know what's going on."

Kimberly and Wolf both nodded their agreement. It was Wolf who quickly left the room to get the other set of parents.

Peter thought silence was his best defense right then. He didn't want to inadvertently start something he didn't need to. Seeing a group of kids go running and screaming past the window, he gave a small sigh. Now that the immediate danger was over, he would rather be out playing with them than continuing this interrogation.

Within minutes, Wolf came back with the family in tow. Catie was all smiles when she saw Peter. That smile faded, however, when she spotted the clues and treasures they had found lined up on Uncle Lance's desk. About to ask him where he had been, she clamped her mouth shut. Sensing the tension in the room, she remained silent and waited to hear what was going on as she sat down next to Peter on the sofa.

Getting Lance's okay, Wolf gave a very quick run-down on all that had happened since Peter had left Catie earlier that afternoon. He also told Beth and Adam a little about the treasure hunt the two kids were on. Both Peter and Catie were surprised by the lack of shock they would have expected to see on Adam and Beth.

"Honey, why didn't you tell us?" was Beth's first question to her daughter. "You know you can tell us anything. Maybe we could have helped prevent some of this."

"Because I thought you wouldn't have understood," Catie mumbled, looking down.

"That's what Peter said, too," Kimberly told Beth with a secret smile.

The five adults seemed to be conversing with each other without actually speaking. After about two minutes of silent contemplation with each other, Lance turned to the two kids who were warily watching them. He was amused when they shrank away from him a little. He could tell they were expecting to be in *big* trouble.

"First off," he began, "we're glad you are both all right but we are also understandably upset you have been manhandled and threatened. That *will be* dealt with later. By us," he added and looked at Wolf. "Second," he held up two fingers and gave them an unexpected bright smile, "we understand much better than you think. Because," he paused dramatically, seeing the two kids lean forward on their seats, "we all—well, with the exception of Wolf here—we all have been involved in something quite similar to what you two have been doing."

He let that sink in for a couple of minutes. Peter and Catie looked at each other, confused. Peter took the lead. "What do you mean? When?"

Lance went over to Catie's parents and put a fond hand on their shoulders. "Adam, Beth and myself found ourselves immersed in what we considered to be one of Walt's Hidden Mickey quests, gosh, what was it? Twelve? Thirteen years ago?"

"It was before we were married," Beth thought back, looking at Adam. "Fifteen years? Has it really been that long?"

"And then your dad and I found another clue that put us on another quest right after that." Kimberly took Lance's hand when he went over to join her. "That's where we fell in love and got married shortly after."

"Ah," Catie smiled and sighed. "That's so romantic."

Peter looked at her like she was crazy. "Romantic? Getting shoved around and your head banged against a wall? What's romantic about that!?"

"What head banging?"

"Who banged who against a wall?"

"What are they talking about?"

"Did you leave out something that we need to know about?"

"Oops," Peter mumbled when the conversation suddenly veered back to his painful adventure with Todd.

Wolf stepped in, glad the ramifications of the previous quests were glossed over. There were some things they didn't want the kids knowing about just yet—some things even Adam and Beth didn't know about. Holding up a quieting hand, he stopped the barrage of questions. "Todd, as of this minute one of my *ex*-security men," he quickly explained for Adam and Beth's benefit, "somehow followed the kids and got a little rough with Peter. We're still not sure how he knows as much as he apparently does. It was as if he was following Peter everywhere he went, or, somehow listening in on all their conversations."

"Then that has to be the security guy who followed Peter into Pirates that day," Beth figured out. "Todd something-or-other. I knew there was something about him I didn't like. What I don't get is how could he have been here at the party all day and I didn't see him?"

Wolf gave a small growl. He blamed himself for part of this mess. "There seems to be a lot about the man that we didn't know. He appears to be pretty adept at staying in the background, out of sight."

Beth shook her head, frustrated that she hadn't spotted him. Getting back to her original train of thought, she added, "When he came to me at the unloading dock in Pirates, he had Peter's backpack but wouldn't hand it over. Then, when enough time had passed to make it obvious that Peter had jumped from the ride, he left."

"At the blue tunnel?" Adam asked, turning to Peter, a small smile tugging at the corners of his mouth.

"How come everyone knows about that tunnel?" Peter exclaimed, looking baffled.

"Yeah, that's where I figured he went when he didn't come back," Beth was nodding to Adam as they all ignored Peter's frustrated question.

Peter looked at Catie and shook his head in disbelief. The one part that he really expected to get yelled at they weren't concerned about at all. *Parents. Can't ever figure them out.*

"Uncle Wolf?" Knowing he wouldn't get any answers, Peter suddenly thought of something else. "If Todd knew everything, why was he demanding the answer to the last clue? I kinda saw that he didn't know where to go next."

They all had to stop and think on that question. Wolf paced the room. "He always seemed to know exactly where you were going to be, right? When did that stop?"

Peter gave a shrug. "The last clue was in my backpack. He still had the pack after we got away. But," he brightened, remembering something important, "he only had a partial clue! I had the whole thing written on my hand."

"Did you always have the backpack with you?"

"Yeah, it's my school pack. I take it everywhere."

"Did you have it when you first encountered Todd?" Wolf wanted to know.

Peter shrugged. "In the Tiki Room? Yeah, but he never touched it. He just put his hands on our shoulders and got Michael and me out of the room."

Wolf couldn't see an answer. "I don't know. We'll probably never figure it out. I doubt he will tell us."

"What do we do next?" Adam wanted to know. "I don't want to allow either Peter or Catie to be put in any more danger. This quest of theirs will have to stop."

"Dad!"

"Uncle Adam!"

"I agree with Adam."

"We're not done yet!"

"Uncle Wolf!"

"Mom!"

"It's too dangerous!"

It was again Wolf who stepped in. "Hold on!" he said in his deep voice. All six participants in the debate stopped. "I agree with Peter and Catie." He held up a hand again as the parents were all ready to jump into the fray again. "Hold it. Now, I don't want them to get hurt any more than you do. *You know that*," he stressed and stared at each parent in turn. Backing down, they each had to nod in agreement. "Knowing that, you each also know how important these Hidden Mickey quests are to the ones running them." Again he stopped and stared at the four adults.

"But they're so young…," Kimberly started.

"Age has nothing to do with it," Wolf cut her off. "You, of all people, should know the long-range idea Walt had in mind when he set these quests in motion so long ago. They don't," he indicated the wide-eyed pair still sitting side-by-side on the sofa. "But, it might have a profound effect on their future. As. It. Did. Yours," he finished pointedly, including all of the adults in the room in his statement.

He didn't need to say any more. Adam and Beth thought about the way they had found each other again and the way they were able to use the treasure they had uncovered. There had been ongoing donations to charities and multiple art scholarships. Adam had been able to fund a low-income housing development he had always wanted to do that was proving to be a tremendous benefit to the community. Lance and Kimberly reflected on the way their quest had brought them together and how they were now married. And—unknown to Adam and Beth—they had also become the next Guardians of Walt.

Looking at Wolf, Lance narrowed his eyes. Was Wolf going to go there? Was he planning on revealing their respective roles?

Seeing his inquiring, silent look and understanding its import, Wolf gave Lance a brief shake of his head. That information was for Lance and Kimberly to disclose, if and when they saw fit. In all this time, no one had mentioned the War Room upstairs. It seemed to have been forgotten with all that had been disclosed and the danger Peter had been in.

"Wolf, we need to know definitely that Peter and Catie will be safe. I don't think even you can assure us of that."

Wolf looked over at Kimberly. He wanted to promise her that nothing bad would ever happen to Peter or Catie again. But, realistically, he couldn't. He could try and take Todd out of the picture, but doubted the man was still at his apartment or even in Southern California by now, for that matter. What he could assure her was that Todd would no longer be working for Disneyland's Security Department. That was a given. Even Todd would recognize that he had just blown his job out of the window. "I know this quest," he quietly told her. "I was with Walt when he set it up."

Out of the corner of his eyes, he could see Adam and Beth's mouths open to ask how that was possible. Walt had been gone for over four decades. "Not now," he simply told them, silencing the obvious question. Sensing something of greater import was going on here, their mouths snapped shut and they became silent observers.

Wolf continued. "There is only one more step to this quest. You know *where* to go, right, Peter?"

Taken aback when everyone suddenly

turned to look at him, Peter just mutely nodded.

Satisfied, Wolf walked over to Lance's desk and picked up one of the keys. "But you don't yet know the entry where these work. That is your final task." He turned back to face the parents before he continued, "They need to finish it. I'll be there when Todd comes—as we know he will." He held up a restraining hand to the objections that were about to fly at him again. "He won't give up until it's over, and he knows he needs these keys. Since we don't want him coming back here to the house, we have to move quickly. I will be there, in the shadows, waiting for him."

"We'll be there, too," Lance firmly stated, saying what each of the other parents was thinking.

Wolf wasn't too sure that was a good idea. "If he sees you all, he might take off and I won't be able to grab him and do what I need to do."

Kimberly looked steadily at their friend. "You have a plan." She said it as a statement, not a question.

With a nod, he added, "I will take him somewhere he won't bother anyone again."

Kimberly gave a curt nod as a chill went over her arms, knowing full well what that meant. Lance saw her rubbing her arms and came over to take her hand. "Like Daniel," she whispered, much to the confusion of Adam and Beth and the children.

"There are too many questions remaining for that not to happen," Lance quietly told her, his eyes briefly darting upwards towards the ceiling.

Knowing he was indicating the still-undis-closed War Room, Kimberly nodded. She could see no other way. Her family and that treasured secret could not be threatened.

Trying to divert the tension that had deep-ened in the room, Wolf turned to Adam. "Did you ever tell Catie about your father working for Walt?"

"What? Really, Daddy? Grandpa John knew Walt Disney?" Catie's eyes got really wide and the delighted smile on her face was like a ray of sunshine that suddenly split the clouds overhead.

Staring for a brief moment at the security guard, Adam let Wolf have his way even as he wondered how Wolf knew his family history. He would ask the piercing questions at a later time—and he would get some answers. "Yes, honey, he did," he answered, turning back to his daughter. "Well, he worked for Disneyland, ac-tually, not specifically Walt. He was working on the Haunted Mansion when it was being built."

"I didn't know that!" Beth exclaimed, lean-ing back to look into his face. "You never men-tioned it."

Adam gave a good-natured shrug. "Don't know why not, actually. He was working in a lot of different departments in his effort to get his contractor's license. He was doing electrical work on the Mansion. I do remember him telling me that Walt came up to him one day to ask about something for the train in his yard, but Walt got diverted by something on the ground.

After he picked up a piece of electrical tubing, Walt asked him about it…." Adam's voice faded away. Suddenly understanding what he had just revealed, he looked off into the distance, his sentence unfinished.

"What's the matter, honey?" Beth asked, patting his hand. "What else did Walt say?"

Adam's head snapped back to face her. At that moment, he had just figured out that the tubing Walt had questioned his dad about was the same tubing in which each of his and Lance's Hidden Mickey clues had been found. He shot a quick, questioning glance at Wolf, but found his face unreadable. "Um, there wasn't much more," he finished, clearly distracted. "Walt never did say what he wanted for his train. He wished my dad a happy marriage, which really surprised Dad because he didn't think Walt had never met my mom…." Adam broke off again, looking over at Lance and Kimberly. They had wide-eyed expressions on their faces, like they knew, but didn't know. "That's all," he finished quietly when no one else said anything.

"Wow, that's really cool!" Catie exclaimed, inadvertently breaking the mood that had just fallen over the room. "I'll have to ask Grandpa John about that next time I see him!"

Wolf looked out at the expanse of the back yard he could see through the window. "I think you all need to get back to the party. The natives are getting restless. It looks like one of the umbrella tables is now set up in the middle of the pool."

"Oh, dear," exclaimed Kimberly, jumping up

to look for herself. She let out a small laugh. "There are four of them sitting at the table like they're expecting a waitress to come by and take their order!" She gave a sudden sigh and turned back to the room, her face serious once again. "I vote that we trust Wolf and let this play out. He will do everything he can to protect the kids. I know he will."

One by one, though not completely agreeing with her, the other parents reluctantly gave their consent.

With that decision made, they all filed out to return to the party. There were still hours to go before it would wind down and everyone would go home.

Lance and Wolf were the last to leave the study. Lance put a firm hand on Wolf's arm. "I know you treat Peter like he was your own son. Do what you have to do to protect them."

"I will."

Lance stared into Wolf's blue eyes for a long moment. Satisfied, with a final nod of trust, he turned and left the study, shutting the door quietly behind him.

CHAPTER 12

Constantly checking his rearview mirror for any sign of Wolf's red Mustang catching up with him, Todd sped down Brea Boulevard as he headed for the relative safety of the Imperial Highway. Once he was on the highway, he could speed up even more and put a greater distance between him and his pursuer—because he knew his car wouldn't stand a chance in an all-out race against Wolf's classic '67 Mustang GT.

Swerving in and out of traffic, Todd's white-knuckle grip on his steering wheel didn't relax until he hit his off-ramp in Brea and still saw no sign of pursuit. Not wanting to call attention to himself and his broken window by getting a speeding ticket, he kept to the posted speed as he headed to his apartment through the city streets. Glancing at the shards of glass covering his passenger seat, a chill went through him as he realized how close he had come to getting caught.

The expense of repairing the window didn't bother him. He had plenty of stolen credit cards and cash on hand for that. No, it was the look of Wolf's face, those eerie blue eyes filled with hatred that caused Todd's forehead to break out in a sweat. Screeching to a stop in his parking stall, Todd had to hold himself back from actually running through the apartment complex to the safety of his rooms. Once the front door was slammed shut and the deadbolt in place, Todd began to breathe more evenly, his back pressed against the door.

But, he knew, deep down, that if Wolf wanted to get in through that door...he would.

Working as fast as his limited computer knowledge would allow him, Todd tried desperately to figure out the meaning of the **Cour d'A** on the slip of paper he had gotten from Peter. Unlike Peter, he hadn't learned the tricks of the search engines and was left completely frustrated and angry. Even the Gold Pass and the papers he had stolen from the kid and the knowledge of that secret room upstairs in the mansion didn't bring him any calm. Yes, he had plenty of leverage now to use against the Brentwood family and make it quite profitable for himself. But, not fully realizing what he had stumbled upon, he sensed something *bigger* in what Peter was doing and wanted to focus on just that. The Brentwood's secret could just wait a while longer. He wanted to know what the boy was doing and he wanted whatever it was that the boy would find.

He just couldn't figure out the clue that Peter had written down. He needed help.

Pushing away from his computer, Todd tried to rid his mind of the look on Wolf's face as he threw that rock. That image was blocking Todd's attempts to come up with a plan—a plan that didn't include Wolf's huge hands wrapped around his neck and squeezing….

Okay, that isn't helping, he thought, running a shaky hand through his messy brown hair. *Who can help? I don't even have to be told to know I am fired from Disneyland. Who can I call for a favor?*

Running through the list of his friends on the security team, he came up with a very short list. Having a secret profession—that of a thief—made it impractical for him to form deep friendships among those who would, technically, be on the lookout for someone just like him…. Todd could only come up with two names—Tom and Steve. He quickly dismissed Tom. Too squeaky clean and by-the-book. Tom would never assist with what Todd was going to ask.

Steve, on the other hand, might just be perfect. Todd sat a little straighter in his chair as he started to formulate a plan. Thinking about Steve's personal life, Todd knew he had a fiancée named Lori. He couldn't personally see the attraction, but that didn't matter. A small smile started in the corner of Todd's mouth. Lori was a very jealous person. She clamped onto Steve wherever they went. However, he didn't recall seeing her at the Brentwood party with

Steve today. Steve was there alone. Todd's smile deepened as he remembered something else: Steve didn't remain alone at the party. Wendy, his ex-girlfriend, was there and they were apparently having a fun time of it in the pool. *Too bad I hadn't brought my camera*, he thought ruefully. And just as fast as he had that thought, another brilliant idea came to his mind: Steve didn't know he hadn't brought a camera....

Leaning forward in his chair, Todd was picturing the scene as it played out in his head. If Steve didn't go along with his 'request,' it would not go well with Lori. Glancing at the clock on his faded walls, Todd figured he should wait until tomorrow. That would give Steve plenty of time at the on-going party with Wendy today and then have Sunday with his fiancée. Around four o'clock in the afternoon should be a good time to give Steve a call.

"**A**re you blackmailing me?" Steve couldn't believe his ears. Having lowered his voice to a whisper after he heard Todd's request, Steve had gone out onto his patio, away from Lori's inquisitive ears. "Is that what you're saying, Todd? We're supposed to be friends, man."

"And, as a friend, I asked for your help and you said no," Todd calmly pointed out. "I just can't accept that as your final answer."

"I'm NOT going to spy on Wolf for you! I don't have a death wish, you know. That's absurd."

"All you have to do is tell me where he takes

those kids. That's all. I know they will show up at Disneyland some time tomorrow and I just need to know where he takes them inside the Park. I can't watch every part of the Park at the same time," he added, leaving out the part about his being more-than-likely fired from the force.

"I don't care. Do it yourself," Steve hissed at him, looking over his shoulder to see where Lori was. "I can't believe you would tell Lori about Wendy! Nothing happened. We were just talking."

Todd gave a sigh like you would give to a child who didn't understand a simple command. "Now, Steve, you know that and I know that, but pictures don't lie. Do you think Lori would like an eight-by-ten glossy or a couple of wallet-sized shots to keep with her forever?"

"This is bogus, man. I can't believe you're doing this to me." An unfamiliar feeling of hatred wormed its way through Steve. He pulled the phone away from his ear and contemplated hurling it into the bushes. But, that would solve nothing. "This ends it between you and me, Todd," he said with finality. "I'll do it because I have to, but never, NEVER speak to me or Lori again. You got that?"

Todd gave a smug grin that came across the phone line. "Yeah, I got that, Steve. You just let me know where Wolf ends up with the brat and you're off the hook. Even though you're still stuck with Lori," he gave as a final dig before shutting his phone and ending the call.

Todd's phone rang earlier on Monday than he expected. Being a school day, he figured Peter and Catie would get to Disneyland much later in the day. It seems, though, that they were kept out of school.

"Steve! How's life treating you?" he asked cheerily when he answered the ring.

"Cut the pleasantries, Todd," Steve snapped at him in a hushed voice. "I still don't like this."

"Fine, have it your way. Where are they? How long have they been inside?"

"Hey, was that the Monorail horn? Where are you, Todd?"

"At the main gate, waiting for you to do what you're supposed to. So, give me my report."

"And then you will destroy the pictures, right?" Steve asked, the urgency and desperation in his voice coming through.

"Right. Just like I promised," Todd smiled to himself. "So? I'm getting bored here."

There was a long pause. It went against everything Steve believed in. He finally gave a deep sigh. "Wolf brought two kids in with him about half an hour ago. A boy and a girl. I recognize the boy to be Lance's son, as you probably already know. If you do anything to those kids…."

"Don't hurt yourself, Stevie. The kids will be fine. Peter has something of mine that I want back, that's all."

Steve didn't believe him, but had no choice but to finish his report. He knew Wolf was with the kids and that would be protection enough.

"Whatever. They came in the Disney Drive entrance, near the Grand Californian. Wolf made a show of taking them all around the Security Department, that kind of thing. Then they went through the back road toward Indy and the Jungle Cruise. I saw them come out in New Orleans Square."

When Steve stopped talking, Todd waited for more. When there was nothing else, he spat, "So, where in New Orleans Square? Do you expect me to just wander around looking for them?"

Steve hesitated in answering. He could just say they went into some shop or other. But, he didn't want to lose Lori, and if Todd found out he was lying, that could be the end result. "Court of Angels," was his resigned reply.

So, that was what the clue meant, he thought to himself, briefly wondering why he hadn't been able to figure it out for himself. "Thanks." Todd snapped the phone shut just as Steve was trying to get his promise again to destroy the pictures. Already on the move, Todd headed up Main Street, a one-day passport in somebody else's name tucked into his shirt pocket.

He just hoped his disguise of a black wig and mustache would be enough to get him close enough to discover the secret the Court of Angels held.

Catie's nerves were calmed somewhat by her excitement of being backstage at Disneyland

in some of the areas where guests are not allowed. Peter, being a frequent visitor with both
his dad and Wolf, was used to the sights, but she
was looking around in wide-eyed wonder. The
horse-drawn trolley had just clomped past her
on its way to duty on Main Street. Wolf told her
how the horse was brought in from the Circle D
ranch behind the Fantasyland area of the Park,
where the trolley was kept, and where the horse
would come out on Main Street right next to the
Fire Station through huge, brightly painted gates
that would swing out. She watched as the huge
brown Belgian horse slowly passed them, unconcerned by all the trucks and delivery vans
going in all directions on the wide path.

"This is so cool!" she gushed to Peter,
touching him on his arm. "Did you see where
they park the Omnibus?"

"What?" Peter was focused on the upcoming search in New Orleans Square and wasn't
paying any attention to what was going on
around him.

"This!" her wide gesture taking in all the activity going on behind the scenes. "What's that
place?" she pointed at a huge green camou-
flaged building.

"Indy," Wolf briefly told her, his eyes busily
scanning for any sign of Todd Raven. Even
though the man was banned from Disneyland,
Wolf knew he could still get in. Hoping their plan
of acting fast and throwing him off the scent
would be successful, there was still a possibility
of danger to the kids. "Come in through here,"
he pointed. "This is where we need to be."

It further delighted Catie that they could be on a busy back street with a Main Street trolley car and various costumed cast members one minute and then, through one corridor, could emerge in the quaint streets of New Orleans Square. "This is so cool!" she repeated. "Can we go back that way again on the way out?"

"We'll see," was Wolf's brief answer as he turned his attention to Peter. "You have the keys?"

Peter, starting to get nervous, bit his lip and nodded without saying anything.

"You have to take it from here, Peter. I can't help you. You have to find what you find."

At Catie's look of worried astonishment that he was actually leaving them alone, he put a calming hand on her shoulder. "I'll be here in the shadows watching. You'll be fine," he promised. "I think we have the element of surprise on our side. Todd shouldn't expect us to move so quickly and you both should be in school. Hopefully you can find the secret today. Your mom is just around the corner working Pirates again, Catie," he tried to reassure her. "It's just a few steps away if you need to go there. Okay?"

"You won't leave us?" she asked in a small voice.

Squatting down, Wolf brought his eyes to her level. "I'll be here, watching. I won't let him hurt you or Peter."

She looked deeply into his blue eyes and gave a short nod.

Turning to face Peter now, Wolf merely stated, "You're on. You know what to do."

"Not really," Peter admitted with a crooked smile. "But, we'll figure it out."

"I'll see you later, then," as Wolf got to his feet and melted into the shadows.

Peter turned to his companion. "You heard him. We're on, Catie. Let's try and figure out where the keys go. You remember what they look like, right?"

With Wolf's assurance and Peter's eagerness, Catie felt her fears begin to fall away. The excitement of the hunt filled her and she looked around the beautiful quiet courtyard. "Yes, but I don't see any keyholes, though."

"Well, we'll just have to look everywhere! You go up the stairs and I'll look under them. Oh, and let me know if you spot anything that looks like a W. E. D."

Catie paused at the base of the blue staircase and looked up the wide, sweeping steps. "But, Peter, this area up here is for cast members only," she hesitated. From their research they had discovered that the stairs lead to at least three different destinations and all of them were for the employees.

"Yeah, I know. One of the doors goes to a storage room for Club 33 and another one goes to the assistant manager's office. I think that's behind those burgundy shutters. I wouldn't knock on that one, if I were you," he tried to kid but immediately saw the resulting stricken look that came over her face. "Catie, it's okay to walk up the stairs. We aren't going in anywhere unless we see that the keys fit. Oh, and if you keep going, there are stairs that, I think, take you down into the Pirates building—which I would love to check out," he added more to himself.

As she slowly started up the stairs, she had to ask, "What was it again you said to look for? Wed what?"

Peter was already looking over the paned doorway leading into one of the shops, running his hand over the smooth painted woodwork. "Hmmm? No, the initials W, E, and D. That's what I found at the Studio. I don't know if it would be the same here, though. Just something else we have to keep in mind."

Nodding, the girl continued upwards, stopping where the stairway turned to check out the statue that Walt had found in Paris. Hesitant to touch it, she stepped closer and looked into the shadowy curve of the wall behind it. Pushing aside some of the greenery, she didn't see any keyholes or any initials.

Looking up, she could see balconies overhead, accessible from the inside only, but there were no obvious places for keys there, either. Continuing, her heart started to pound a little as she approached the landing at the top. Right in the middle of the landing was a standing oval sign that read *Cast Members Only Please*. She was about to call down to Peter, but she couldn't see him. Going past the warning sign, she turned away from the door on the left and tiptoed down the landing, examining all woodwork and doorways as she continued.

After checking out the keyhole in the burgundy door where Todd had first held him, Peter quickly moved to a different part of the courtyard.

He was out of her sight because he was directly beneath her, under the staircase. He had found a wooden panel door in the wall that had a simple round handle and a spring to keep it closed, but it was obvious his keys would not fit the small brass lock.

Giving an uninterested, "Hmph," he stood back and looked around the small courtyard, hands on his hips. There were two entries into the Court of Angels from the New Orleans Square streets. The largest, most often used corridor was the one facing Orleans Street. The second entrance was currently more or less blocked by an artist doing chalk portraits of guests. There were numerous easels set up with canvases that displayed her finished work. The easels were arranged in a way that limited the view into the courtyard. Peter was glad to see that. One less place for interruption should they find something.

There were also two shops that had rear exits into the courtyard. The woodwork on each exit door was painted in the same blue as the staircase and the balconies. However, these doors were currently closed as it wasn't busy enough in the Park just yet to warrant having two entrances and exits. Peter didn't even bother looking at the doors of the other shop across from him. Any key that fit those doors would just allow entrance into the shop and he couldn't see that as being the answer for which he was searching.

Likewise unimportant to Peter were the white wrought iron benches placed here and there around the shady nook. He could see they were easily moveable and would have no hidden secrets. Glancing up to the staircase to see how his partner was doing, he saw Catie was currently examining something on the wall. Knowing she would call him if it were important, he quickly scanned the area she had already covered.

The curved nook with the statue caught his eye with its two hanging gas lanterns that gave it a lovely flickering effect at night. He would ask Catie later if she had gone over every inch of the base.

There was a plaque on the wall, but, from his research, he knew it was added to the wall many years after Walt's time. It was a special tribute to a long-time cast member who had suddenly died. Listing her name, it also said Musique des Anges—music of angels—and offered music lessons and vocal instructions. This was a fitting acknowledgement as she had sung in a choir. The plaque was a nice alternative to the glass windows on Main Street that were awarded to special people who had contributed to Disneyland.

At the sudden sound of a door opening upstairs, Peter quickly threw himself onto the seat of the closest bench and pretended to be fascinated by whatever was in the shop window next to him. The oblivious cast member who had been prepping inside Club 33 trotted down the stairs, apparently not having seen Catie. Peter waited until the server had vanished around the corner of Royal Street and then smiled to himself when he heard Catie let out a huge sigh of relief.

Peter now turned his attention to the beautiful tan and cream marble backdrop of the fountain. Built into the wall under the staircase, it had a solid marble bench that curved around the half-moon shaped pool into which the clear blue water splashed and rippled. Delicate green ferns filled rounded urns on each end of the bench. In the center of the diamond-shaped stonework that formed the backsplash, a small nozzle protruded, its tip shaped like the petals of a tulip as the water trickled into the waiting pool. When Peter leaned in for a closer look, his eyes widened. For there, concealed in the layers of the design, were the lightly carved initials **W.E.D**. Excited, he reached out a tentative finger to touch the letters, but pulled his hand back. In case this was it, Catie should be here for whatever might happen.

Standing back, he located her on the opposite side of the long walkway. By the set of her shoulders, he could tell she was discouraged by not finding anything yet. Softly whistling, he got her attention and motioned for her to come down. Visibly relieved by his summon, she hurried back to the curving staircase.

"Did you find something?" she eagerly asked when she reached his side. "I haven't found anything but dust," she exclaimed, holding up her dirt-covered fingertips to prove her point.

Just then, two guests slowly wandered into the court. Catie and Peter, trying not to look guilty, dropped onto the nearest bench. Watching out of the corners of their eyes, they saw the couple was taking pictures of each other posing on the stairs. Seeing the two kids, the woman approached and, smiling, held out her camera to the oldest, Peter. "Would you mind taking a picture of the both of us, please? It's our anniversary! Just push that button," she pointed.

"Uh, sure," Peter said slowly, getting to his feet as she happily trotted back to her husband and they climbed up three stairs together. Aiming the small digital camera, he centered them in the frame. After snapping the picture, he handed it back to the appreciative woman. "You might want to check it first before you go. I'm not very good with a camera."

The woman smiled at the boy and hit a couple of buttons. "Thanks! It's perfect." She held it out for Peter to see, but could quickly tell he wasn't really interested. "Thanks again," she grinned as she slid her arm through her husband's and they wandered back out into New Orleans Square.

Once they were out of sight, Catie jumped up from the bench and came over to Peter. "What did you find? What did you find?"

"Here, sit on the bench in case anyone comes in again," he pointed to one side of the marble seating area under the fountain. He sat on the other side and pointed. "What do you see here?"

Catie had to lean in really close to see the initials. "Gosh, is that what you meant? What does it mean? You never did tell me."

"It's Walt's initials, but it was also one of his companies," Peter explained as he stared at the letters that Walt probably carved out himself.

"How do you remember so much?" she asked in awe. "I can't remember half of the stuff we researched."

Her companion could only shrug. "My dad's the same way. We can remember almost everything we read. Comes in handy in school," he added with a charming smile.

"So what do we do now? I don't see any keyhole."

"Yeah, I know. I didn't see one, either," Peter sighed and tried peering into the shadowy corners beyond the courtyard. "Wish Wolf would tell us. Maybe we should feel around this diamond shape and see if there is a hidden hole of some kind."

"You do it," she whispered, anxious. "I'll…I'll keep watch."

"Okay. Then you should stand in front of me and block the way. I don't want anyone to think I'm messing with the fountain."

Catie didn't like it that she wouldn't be able to see what he was doing, but did as he asked. Within seconds she could hear a startled gasp from Peter and the grating noise of stone rubbing against stone. Whirling around, she could see the entire inner portion of the arched marble stonework pulling backwards into the wall. The water from the fountain, however, still shot outwards, reaching farther and farther as it continued to land in the middle of the small pool. When a dark entrance was revealed, the movement of the wall stopped, apparently waiting.

"What did you do?" she exclaimed, staring at the hole.

"That's it! We found the secret door, Catie," Peter exclaimed, grabbing his new backpack off his shoulders and digging around in it for a flashlight. "Come on, before it closes."

"I don't want to go in there!"

"We have to, Catie. This has to be it. Come on, we have to hurry before anyone sees us."

Clicking his flashlight on, Peter stepped over the pool of water and crawled through the narrow entrance. Swallowing, Catie took one last, desperate look around hoping to see Wolf coming to join them. Seeing no one and fighting back her fears, she had no choice but to follow the sliver of light that would be Peter.

As soon as she had crawled through the opening, both Peter and Catie were startled when the entry door slid shut behind them. Except for the one small beam of light, they were in total, musty darkness.

CHAPTER 13

"They did it!" Wolf grinned as he stepped out from his hiding place once the marble slid back into place. He had seen Catie's anxious glance and knew she had been looking for him. Sorry he was not able to allay her fears, he understood how important it was for them to continue by themselves. Still, pride came through when he muttered, "I knew Peter had it in him. Hope he brought more than one flashlight. He's going to need it," he smiled to himself as he headed for the exit of Pirates. He wanted to let the girl's worried mother know that the kids had made their discovery and that they were safe.

As soon as the security guard walked off, Todd Raven came out of his own hidden corner. He had been tucked away in the dark entrance to a closed shop during this entire time. Knowing where Wolf had been stationed, it had been easy for him to melt out of view and still be able to watch.

Walking swiftly to the bench on the wall, he

hesitated as he pulled off the scratchy, irritating disguise. Stuffing the black wig and beard into the nearest potted plant, he stood staring at the elaborate design of the fountain. As far away as he had been hiding, and with the girl partially blocking his view, he wasn't exactly sure what the kid had done to open the secret panel. "Couldn't have been too difficult if the brat figured it out," he mumbled as he pushed on every square inch of the wall within the general area that had captured Peter's interest. When it was obvious that his actions were not working, he started to look for some kind of hidden lever. Feeling all over the raised design, he could find nothing unusual.

Not knowing how long Wolf would be gone, Todd knew that just standing there and staring at the wall wouldn't work. He had to figure it out and follow those two kids and fast. It was his only chance.

As soon as the darkness closed over them, Peter felt an anxious hand grab his leg. They were both still crouched down from crawling into the opening. "Is that you, Catie?"

That earned him a chuckle, breaking the scared mood that had descended over them. "Who else would it be? You have someone else in here that I don't know about?"

The orange beam of light swung around and illuminated her smiling face. "Yeah, it's you," Peter grinned, his own features lost in the gloom. Handing her the light, he added, "Hold this. I

have another one in my pack. Always be prepared, you know."

As he fiddled with the unfamiliar backpack,
the light was swung away from him as Catie tried
to see what was in the darkness around them.
"Hey, I can't see in my pack. Shine it over here."

"Oh, sorry," as the beam lit up the bright red
backpack again. "Do you have any idea where
this leads?"

"Not exactly. I think there's a passage off
to the left. At least, I think that's what I saw before you grabbed me. Maybe a staircase?"

"Does it go up or down?" she asked, hoping
he would say up.

"Well, if that is what it was, it was probably
up."

"Oh, good." She sounded relieved for some
reason.

"Why is that good?"

"Down is always scary! Don't you watch
any movies?"

Peter gave a chuckle. Catie always surprised him. "I think down would lead us somewhere near The Pit restaurant and the underside
of Pirates. Even though that would be really fascinating and I am hungry, I have no idea where
either a hallway or stairs would take us. You
ready? I have the other light."

Two matching beams of light came now into
play and pointed forward into the unknown
blackness. With the added help of Catie's flashlight, they could see it was an extremely narrow
passage that was just barely tall enough to walk
upright. As they got to their feet, they both in-

stinctively knew it was time to remain as quiet as possible.

It came as a surprise to Catie when Peter suddenly whispered, "Stay close." He immediately felt her hand searching for his. "Here," he offered, shining his light briefly to show where his free hand was. Feeling her warm grasp, he turned back to the passage. "You ready? It's pretty narrow. Eww."

"Shh! What?"

Catie heard a loud smack on the wall. "Nothing," he whispered over his shoulder as he began to move slowly forward. Catie tried to avoid looking at all the cobwebs that hung down from the unseen ceiling.

After inching along the side wall for about ten feet, the flashlights seemed to show a dead end as a cement wall loomed in front of them. Not giving up, they kept moving forward until they found the angled corner of the courtyard. Just a few feet more beyond the corner, the wall suddenly curved inwards toward them. "I know where we are!" Peter looked back at her, talking in an excited, hushed voice as he took another couple of steps forward. "This is that place on the stairs with the statue of the boy. Remember? Oww!"

"What happened? Are you hurt?" Catie hurriedly whispered, hoping it wasn't serious so she would have to figure out where to go for help.

If Peter had had a free hand he would have rubbed his bruised knee. "I'm okay. I hit my knee on…something metal, I think. It sure felt like metal." He broke off as both of their flashlights did what they should have been doing all along—pointing at what was in front of them instead of what was above. "Oh, wow, it's a spiral staircase! How come I didn't see that coming?"

"Because you were looking at me?"

Peter could hear the smile in her voice. He almost replied that it was because she was prettier than the plain walls around them, but suddenly decided not to. Instead, he set his foot on the first step and shined his light up into complete darkness. Trying to sound like Peter Pan, he whispered, "Come on, everybody! Here we go!" He was rewarded by a light chuckle.

They counted twenty steps as they climbed higher and higher into the unknown. The walls surrounding them, just as they had been in the passageway, were made of plain white concrete and undecorated. The handrail was black iron and also unadorned.

"Compared to outside, it's not very pretty in here," Catie mumbled as her light illuminated the bland features around them.

"I guess all that matters is what we find at the top. Hey, I think we're there!"

Catie could hear the excitement in his voice. "What is it? What did you find? Is there room for me?" Her light was only showing Peter's backpack and the walls. The staircase was so narrow it allowed only one of them on a step at a time. She wondered if it would be the same at the top landing.

She noticed Peter pointed his light at the landing at his feet. It, too, looked narrow and dusty. "Not sure. There might only be room for me, I think. Sorry." When his ray of light moved around the landing, it lit up what appeared to be a door. Close enough now, he could tell that it was painted the same blue as the woodwork outside in the Court of Angels.

As Peter stepped onto a wider landing than he had expected, he turned to face the door. Because she was still standing lower than Peter on the stairs, Catie let go of his hand and immediately clasped onto the dusty banister of the staircase. Her flashlight began exploring.

"Peter, what's that?" Her light was shining above his head into the corner of the small alcove.

"Where? Oh, up there? I don't know. See that red dot? Is that some kind of camera? Wonder where it goes?"

Still one step below him, Catie couldn't see everything. "I don't know. Did you find a door? Is there a lock? Tell me what you see!"

At her request, Peter moved his beam of light back to the blue door and forgot all about what might have been a camera. As he carefully examined the door in front of him, neither one of them noticed when the red light above them turned green.

"Lance!" Kimberly excitedly exclaimed as she sat far away in Fullerton, "They found it! They're at the door to the chamber."

Lance hurried across the War Room to the bank of monitors that Kimberly had been watching. Turning a button on one of the screens, the wavering image of Peter and a beam of light behind him that must be Catie came into sharper focus. "That's my boy," Lance muttered.

"*Our* boy!" Kimberly corrected him, obviously proud of their son. "Imagine. Our son is following in our footsteps. This might not be the secret chamber we found above Main Street, but I'm so happy to see that they have followed each clue that Walt had put in place. Wow, Lance! Peter might be our successor as Guardian," she smiled at Lance, her eyes getting a little misty.

"What about Catie?" asked Lance, watching as they saw Peter fumbling with the keys, trying to figure out how they worked. "She's in on this, too."

"Yeah, I know. Well, we'll just have to wait and see how this plays out," she shrugged. "Catie's parents didn't pursue anything once they found the first treasure. It took you digging deeper to find that it went further. I don't know how she will react to all of this."

As they continued to stare at the monitor, they both wondered what the eleven-year-old girl and the thirteen-year-old boy would do with their futures that were about to be changed forever.

"I can't get the key to work, Catie," Peter told her, frustrated and getting warm in the close darkness.

"Why not? Doesn't it fit?"

"It kinda fits, but it's wobbly and the teeth won't grab," he tried to explain.

"Did you try the other key, too?"

"Yeah, both of them do the same thing."

"Is there another keyhole we haven't seen yet? Maybe you have to use one of the keys in each hole. Do you think?" she wondered, her flashlight going up to the top of the doorway.

Peter's light joined hers and then took a slow journey to the bottom of the doorframe. "No, there's no other keyhole. This has to be the right one."

"Want me to try?" came the timid offer. She didn't want to make Peter feel like he couldn't do it right, but it was difficult to just stand there and do nothing.

"Sure," came his immediate response. He was relieved, actually, and welcomed her help. "You'll have to squeeze up here, though. Don't drop the keys! I don't want to have to climb all the way down there again."

With slightly shaky hands, Catie accepted the two keys after handing her flashlight to her companion. She then slid her slender body into the small space between Peter and the door. Under different circumstances, she might have enjoyed the close proximity to Peter, but this was not the time. "You're right. They don't seem to fit very well. Gosh, I hope this isn't the wrong location. Do you think there's another secret passage?"

"There are probably a lot of secret passages we don't know about. But, all the clues pointed to this place. The keys have to work. Try the other one," he suggested, peering over her shoulder as he aimed the light at the brass keyhole.

The second key had the same results as Peter had gotten. "Shine your light over the keys, Peter," she requested as she stared at the brass lying in her open hands. "Maybe there's something on them we missed."

The light only showed what Peter had seen before. One side of the key was flat, but it was opposite from its mate.

"Did you ever try to fit them together? Do they match up?"

"Yeah, but they are still two keys."

"Aren't they thicker that way?" she wondered out loud.

Peter's face lit up. "You're right. Maybe that's the problem. Maybe they have to fit into the lock at the same time. Do you want to try that?"

"Sure. I think I can."

It took only moments for the double key to slide into the lock and nestle perfectly inside. "I think that's it, Peter! It's hard to turn, though."

"Probably because it is so old," he muttered. "Let me help you," as he placed his hand over hers. Together they gave the keys a good turn. They could hear the tumblers fall into place in the close confines of the stairwell. The resulting click was very loud.

"We did it!" she said breathlessly, wanting to hug him, but there wasn't room.

"Okay, help me push the door. It seems really heavy for some reason."

Together, both of the kids pushed on what turned out to be a heavy steel door. With their combined efforts it began to slowly swing in-wards.

A whoosh of stale air swept past them as Peter anxiously shined the two lights into the darkness that had opened up in front of them. Taking her flashlight back, Catie grabbed Peter's free hand once again as he took the first step over the threshold. Their two small beams of light did little to dispel the gloom. Feeling on the wall next to them, Peter found a small toggle switch and pushed it upwards.

With an electrical sizzle, a very small old-fashioned red and white globed chandelier flick-ered on overhead. Dust on the glass lights prevented most of the illumination from shining outward. Still, it was enough to show they were in a narrow room, not much bigger than a large walk-in closet. They could see a window on the far wall covered over with a dark drapery. Some wooden crates were also stacked in the small space, all of them with the stencil *Disneyland* painted on the planks facing outward.

In the middle of the room was a small or-nate table that was topped with veined, white marble. It looked like one of the tables from the Lilly Belle. On top, centered on a yellowed doily, was a small glass case. Dust caked the glass dome as the two flashlights played over it. Walk-ing closer, Peter could see something inside that was gold colored. Dropping Catie's clammy hand, he used the edge of his jacket to wipe off some of the dusty film. Bending closer to the table, he could finally see what was inside. "It's another key," he told Catie who was peering over his shoulder.

"Look, there's an envelope tucked under the wooden base. It looks really old."

"Should we open it?" Peter thought out loud.

"I think it's why we're here. I think," she repeated, the doubt obvious in her voice.

"Okay, if you think we should." Peter gently pulled out the envelope out from under the case and carefully opened the flap. It had long since lost its adhesive.

"Out loud," Catie requested with a chuckle, as Peter was obviously reading silently to himself.

"Oh. Sorry."

"*Hi, there!*" he read,

"*I see that you found my secret hiding place in the Court of Angels. Congratulations on figuring it all out. This quest wasn't as difficult as some of my other Hidden Mickey quests are—or were—depending on when you find this.*

"*What you see in front of you is very special and I hope you will take it seriously. There are only two others like it in existence. I have one of them, of course, and my Guardian Wolf has the other one.*

"*This isn't exactly the Key to the City, but it is the Key to Disneyland. This is a master key that will allow you access to any room anywhere you need to go inside Disneyland and my Studio. As a Guardian, you will have to be able to go everywhere necessary to protect my legacy. This key will help speed up the process. I don't want you to have to fool around with a huge key ring in case something needs your immediate attention.*

"Guard the key well. There could be a lot of mischief if it falls into the wrong hands. And, that is what I am trying to avoid.

"You will find some boxes in here as well. Just some trinkets you might enjoy from the early days of my buddy Mickey and of Disneyland. Take good care of them.

"Thank you,

"Walt Disney."

"Oh, Peter, it is from Walt himself! Isn't that wonderful?"

Peter was distracted by what he read and his head snapped to face her. "What did you say? Wonderful? Yeah, it is," he mumbled, going over to the curtained window. Lifting one corner of the dust-encrusted material, he peeked out. "It's the Court of Angels," he explained. "This looks like one of those balconies that came from nowhere."

"Can we open the window? It's awfully dusty in here."

There were six large panes of glass that covered the upper three-quarters of the French doors. The bottom section was painted wood. Peter pressed closer to one of the panes of glass. "Hey, I think we're right over that statue in the curved wall! See where the staircase curves? There's usually people coming and going all the time, but I don't see anyone out there right now. I guess it would be all right."

Handing the fragile letter to the girl, he struggled with the rusty locks that held the doors firmly shut. Once he got them lifted, the doors swung easily inwards. The fresh air was a welcome relief.

"Catie?" he asked, still watching the courtyard for any sign of activity, "what do you think Walt meant by the word guardian? He seemed to be saying that whoever had this key would be some kind of guardian. And he mentioned Wolf, too."

Catie looked back at the key in question. "Yeah, I noticed that, too. I don't see how it could be *our* Wolf. He isn't nearly old enough to have known Walt. I mean, he is *old*, but not that old!" she commented, voicing the same opinion everyone under the age of fifteen had of anyone over the age of twenty-five.

"I know. I was thinking the same thing. It kinda fits what our parents were talking about after that Todd guy grabbed me. When we were in the study? They said something about Wolf and Walt. Maybe we need to ask him."

Whatever Catie was going to say was cut off when a male voice from the doorway smugly said, "Maybe you need to back away from the window and get over here where I can watch you."

"It's that security guy!" Peter's mouth dropped open. "How did you find us?" He looked quickly over his shoulder out into the courtyard, hoping to see Wolf emerging from the shadows. Wolf was supposed to be out there— not this guy. Stepping protectively in front of Catie, he glared at the intruder when he saw the knife Todd was holding out in front of him.

"Oh, isn't that cute. You're protecting your little girlfriend," Todd spat and motioned with the knife. It was a bigger blade than last time. "Get away from that window. Don't make me tell you again, or I start with the girl this time."

Peter put an arm around Catie and guided her toward the opposite side of the table. "You won't touch her!" he shouted, pointing an accusing finger at the smirking man.

"I'll do what I want!"

"**O**h no! Call Wolf. Now!" Kimberly yelled for Lance as she stared unbelievingly at the monitor. "It's Todd."

Turning away from the holographic map of Disneyland and the red light that was now flashing in New Orleans Square, Lance was frantically looking around for the pager. "How did he get in there? I thought Wolf was watching them!"

"He must have thought it was safe when they got inside. He's probably with Beth."

Lance was angrily punching the emergency button that would alert Wolf's walkie talkie. "I don't care what he's doing. He was supposed to watch them…. Wolf! Get back to the courtyard. Todd has the kids!"

"**W**here's my Gold Pass, you thief!" Peter demanded as he tried to divert the attention away from Catie.

Todd was reading over the letter he had snatched from Peter's hands. "That would be *my* Gold Pass, you spoiled brat. My, you and your family are just one big surprise after another. And, Wolf," he said, tsking with his tongue as he tried to continue reading. "Sounds like he has some secrets, too. Which I am sure he will be willing to share with us just to keep you two brats safe."

"What are you going to do with us?"

Todd liked hearing the fear in Peter's voice. It made him feel powerful. "What I should have done that first day. Get rid of you." Angling the letter more towards the light from the window, he grumbled, "It's still so dark in here. Toss me your flashlight. Now!"

Seeing a chance to do something, Peter heaved the light so it rolled closer to the open French doors that led out to the balcony. He hoped at least Catie could get down the spiral staircase and away.

"Brat," Todd mumbled as he walked over to pick up the light. "By the way," he commented mildly as if discussing the weather, "if either one of you takes as much as one step out of this room before I tell you to, the other one loses an ear first. Then I'll decide if the next part will be an eye or a thumb."

Even in the gloom of the room he could see Catie turn pale at his words. Hoping the brat didn't faint so he would have to carry her out of there, Todd quit his tormenting and tried to read the rest of the letter.

With a sudden, angry roar, a furious Wolf launched himself from the doorway into the open-mouthed, shocked Todd. There wasn't even enough time to get his knife up in defense when he found himself hurtling backwards through the open French doors. The force of the impact broke through the wooden railing around the balcony and the two men fell heavily onto the stairway below.

Todd sustained the majority of the impact as Wolf landed on top of him, knocking the air out of his lungs. He could only whimper when Wolf's fist drew back and landed on the side of his face. For Todd, all went black.

Breathing hard, Wolf looked up and could see Peter perilously close to the broken edge of the balcony. "Are you all right, Uncle Wolf?" he asked anxiously. "You're bleeding!"

"I am?" Surprised, Wolf looked down and saw Todd's knife partially embedded in his side. "How'd that happen?" With a painful grunt, he pulled out the tip of the knife and pressed a hand onto the bleeding wound. Realizing the attention the noise of the breaking balcony would attract, Wolf hastily called Kimberly on their secret line and told her to close down this portion of New Orleans Square. He knew she would make just one call and, within minutes, no one would bother them until she gave the all-clear.

Like an acrobat, Peter grasped the edge of the balcony and swung down from the broken woodwork, landing lightly onto the littered steps next to Wolf. "Are you hurt bad, Uncle Wolf? Can I do anything?"

Wolf looked upward with a frown. "You can help Catie down before she hurts herself. I don't want her trying that stunt you just pulled."

"Hey, I'm in gymnastics. That was easy." At the dark look on Wolf's face, Peter clamped his mouth shut and did as he was told.

"Oh, Wolf! I was so glad to see you," she hugged him, careful to avoid the gash in his side that appeared to have quit bleeding. "Is he...is he still alive?"

Wolf seemed to have forgotten the unconscious man who was still beneath him. Getting slowly to his feet, Wolf prodded the prone Todd with the toe of his shoe. "I think so. I didn't hit him that hard."

"You should have," Peter mumbled, looking as if he was going to give Todd a swift kick in the side.

"I'll take care of this, Peter," Wolf snapped, seeing the angry look on the boy's face. "This is my mess to clean up." He gave a brief grimace as a shot of pain raced through him.

"You're hurt. We need to get you to a doctor!"

Wolf forced his face to return to its normal, dour look. "I'm fine, Catie. This is nothing. I've had worse." He mentally went over the gunshots, arrow holes, sword stab, and knifings he had gone through. No, this little poke was nothing.

Getting back to the matter at hand, he picked up his radio and called for two of his trusted security men to bring a blanket and a wheelchair. "I need to get Todd out of sight. There's a place in Critter Country where he won't be discovered," he told the curious kids.

"Under the Hungry Bear?" Peter asked with

a half smile.

"And just how do you know about that place?" Wolf wanted to know, his eyes narrowing.

Peter gave him a shrug. "Everyone knows about that room. It's just that nobody talks about it."

Catie looked at the mess around them. "What do we do about the balcony? I think you broke it…," she trailed off, knowing how funny that sounded.

Wolf gave her a brief smile. "Yeah, I broke it really good. Don't worry. I'll get a team in here within the hour to get it fixed. By tomorrow no one will know it was even damaged." He turned to Peter. "One of you will need to go back into the room and get…what is yours," he finished quietly, still not sure they were unobserved. "All right?"

Peter nodded. He had forgotten about their exciting discovery in all that happened since. "I'll go. There's some…questions the letter raised," he started to say. Then, glancing down at the still-unconscious Todd, he broke off. "But, I'll ask you later about all that."

Wolf knew where the boy had been heading and was glad Peter cut himself off. This was not the time or place. "Catie, I'd like you to go to your mother. I left there at a run and she's probably worried."

Catie wanted to argue because she really wanted to see the hidden room under the Hungry Bear Restaurant, but, she could use a hug from her mother right about now. "Okay," she agreed with a small voice, her face falling.

Knowing what she wanted to see, Wolf gave her a small smile. "Don't worry. I'll show you the hidden room another time. I promise."

He was rewarded with a huge smile. Catie ran through the entranceway and turned right to go to Pirates. She needed a hug so badly.

When Peter came back down, Wolf glanced up at the broken balcony and saw the French doors were closed once again. He was confident Peter made sure all the doors were securely locked, and that the letter and the key would be safely tucked inside his backpack. "Where's Catie?"

"I sent her to her mother," Wolf explained. "She doesn't need to see where I put him."

The conversation broke off when Wolf's two security friends rushed into the courtyard with the wheelchair. Steve handed Wolf the blanket which was then wrapped around the inert body.

"What happened to Todd?" he tentatively asked, looking up at the broken balcony and seeing the blood staining Wolf's uniform, a feeling of dread coursing through him.

"He was where he shouldn't have been. He tried to hurt the kids," was all Wolf told them.

Steve's face paled. He knew something was up with Todd, but he never expected him to go to that length. "Wolf, I have to tell you something. You're not going to like it," he started, wiping a bead of sweat off his forehead. At Wolf's dark stare, he swallowed and continued, "This is all my fault," he hurriedly explained. "Todd was blackmailing me with some photos from the party of me and Wendy. He was going to give them to my fiancée if I didn't tell him."

"Tell him what, Steve? I don't see what this has to do with you."

Steve glared at the unconscious man. "He wanted to know where you were taking the kids today. He figured you would come to the Park and he said Peter had something of his that he wanted back. I…I didn't want to spy on you, but I didn't want to mess things up with Lori."

Wolf's eyes narrowed. "So that's how he knew where we were. I didn't think he was smart enough to figure it out for himself."

"I'm really sorry. I didn't think he would try to hurt the kids."

"I watched Todd during most of the party. I never saw him with any camera."

Steve's face fell. "He was lying to me? That dirty…."

Wolf put a restraining hand on Steve's arm. Like Peter, Steve looked about ready to kick Todd. "He's lied about a lot of things," Wolf mumbled, looking around. "We have to get him out of here. It's up to Peter to accept your apology."

Peter could tell by the look on the security guard's face that he hadn't meant any harm. He just mutely nodded his acceptance of the apology.

Steve gave him a brief smile. "Thanks," and stuck out his hand out to Peter for a shake. He knew now, with Wolf in charge, things would be all right. He didn't envy Todd's position. "I'll push the wheelchair," he offered, knowing exactly where Wolf was taking him.

Motioning for Peter to follow, the group filed out of the closed-off Court of Angels and headed for Critter Country. The room upstairs had been relocked. The secret passageway was closed. The Key to Disneyland was secure in Peter's backpack. And, most importantly, Peter and Catie were safe.

Now, Wolf reflected with a grunt, the questions would begin.

CHAPTER 14

"**W**ow," Lance was saying as he looked at the intriguing piece of brass sitting on the edge of his desk as a watchful Peter hovered close by. "The Key to Disneyland. I don't even have one of those."

"Yeah, only Walt and Wolf and me," Peter grinned. That cocky smile faded when his dad's head shot up. "I mean, if I get to keep it, that is," he finished, uncertain as his eyes sought out his mother for back-up.

Kimberly looked over at Lance from her place on the sofa, her eyebrows raised in question. *Would he get to keep it?* she seemed to be silently asking him. In the relief that followed Peter and Catie's deliverance from Todd Raven, the parents really hadn't had the time to properly discuss what to do next. Then, before they knew it, Wolf had arrived at the house with Peter in tow.

"So, I'm a guardian now?" Peter ventured to ask when the silence seemed to stretch longer and longer. He bit his tongue when all three adults turned to face him. *Maybe I should have just waited and kept my mouth shut*, he thought too late.

Lance came over to his son and put a hand on his shoulder. "Do you know what a guardian is, Pete? Do you know what the duties are?"

"Duties? There are duties?" he echoed, looking from one purposely-blank face to the other. "Uh, there were only a couple of mentions of a guardian in the letters Walt left." Looking over at their silent friend, he stressed, "And he named Wolf every time." There was an obvious question in his statement.

Receiving a brief nod from Lance, it was Wolf who answered Peter's unasked query. "Yes, Walt was referring to me. We worked together for a long time until…until he died back in 1966." Wolf looked away, his blue eyes staring past the walls of the room. "I miss him," he said in a quiet voice, a voice that revealed more loss than he would have liked to expose. Embarrassed, Wolf cleared his throat and continued in his usual straight-forward manner, "He was a brilliant man and had brilliant plans—both for his time and for the future. It's just a shame he couldn't have been around longer to enjoy what he had created."

While the security guard was talking, Kimberly went over to the far wall in Lance's study. Taking a picture off the wall, she brought it over to Peter and held it up in front of him. "Did you ever see this?"

Not sure if it was a trick question, he warily

shrugged. "It's been on the wall for as long as I can remember."

Giving him an amused grin, she explained, "That's not what I meant. Have you ever looked at the picture? I mean, really looked at it?"

Shaking his head no, Peter took it from her and studied the black and white eight-by-ten photograph. "This was taken here in Dad's study," he said as he examined it. "This is Walt Disney," he pointed, "and this is you, Wolf." A frown formed between his eyes as he stared at the image and Peter wondered out loud, "How come you look just the same as you do now?" Looking back at his mom, he added, "I don't know who this other man is."

"That's my dad, Peter." Kimberly smiled fondly as she gazed at the picture of the blond-headed man in the photo—and subtly ignored the other part of Peter's question. "He was your grandfather. He died about two years before you were born." Her voice caught unexpectedly and she had to pause a moment to get her emotions back in check. When she looked back up at the boy, her eyes were shining with unshed tears. "He would have been so proud of you today, Peter. You see," she explained, "he was Walt's first Guardian. He worked very closely with Walt and was chosen to help protect the legacy of the Disney empire."

"Protect it from what? I don't understand why a guardian would be needed."

Lance walked back to his desk and sat. "Well, there are always people who want a piece of what someone else worked hard to attain. Or, people who don't like how something is being run and feel they can do it better."

Thinking about her own uncle, Kimberly added quietly, "And there are people who just don't like Disney and all it stands for. Because of greed, they try to take what someone else owns and turn it to their own profit. That's where we all come in," she indicated the other two adults in the room with a tilt of her chin. "I took over my father's position when he died and worked with Wolf until your dad had proved himself with one, well," she amended, "two of Walt's quests—similar to what you and Catie just did—and then he joined us. That room you saw upstairs is our headquarters. You haven't asked about it yet, but I can just see the questions burning in your eyes!"

"Walt called it the War Room when he designed this house," Wolf added. "Mostly your mom and dad—sometimes I do, too—watch the monitors and the map making sure everything is where it should be. There are specific guides and plans we follow. All changes to the Park have to go by us."

"Wow! So, the Imagineers call and talk to you?" Peter wanted to know, fascinated at what he was learning.

The three adults didn't answer him right away. "Let's just say that we know what's going on," Lance offered as a bypass for the boy's direct question. "We only act if it is something against the way things should go. I guess I should add something about the secrecy and how no one outside of this room knows our positions. It is *vital* it remains that way," he stressed, getting an affirmative nod from Wolf and Kimberly.

"Man!" Peter whistled, trying to take it all in. "And I'm part of that now! What about Catie?"

"Hold on there, buddy," Lance held up a hand. "There's a lot more at stake and we don't know that you are quite ready for it all." When he saw the boy's face fall, he added, "Son, I didn't say you *wouldn't* be part of it." After glancing at his two partners, he told Peter, "How about this? I vote that we promote you to Junior Guardian status and see how things develop as you get older. It is possible you wouldn't want the position and all it entails when you're an adult." He could see Peter was about to argue with that and he held up his hand again to stave off whatever he was going to say. "Hold on. Let me finish. I know you love the Park and your knowledge of its history is great. But, there's a lot more to it than just that. It takes a huge dedication and commitment. Plus, there are things that have to be given up because of the secrecy. Wolf? Kimberly? Do you two agree with my recommendation?"

Wolf gave one nod of his head and Kimberly agreed as well. "Then, Junior Guardian it is," she smiled to herself, thinking that Lance would have made a wonderful lawyer like his father had wanted him to be.

Seeing things take off in a better direction than it seemed just moments before, Peter eagerly eyed the brass object still sitting on the desk. "So, I get to keep the key then?"

Wolf stepped in and answered for the parents. "I'll take charge of the key for now."

"Hey, you already have one!"

Peter was immediately silenced by the look Wolf gave him. "As your dad said, there is a lot of responsibility that comes with this key. It is a master key that opens every door in Disneyland and the Studio…. Lance, tell you what. Why don't you hang on to this one and at least Peter will know it is in his house. Deal?" Seeing the expression that came over Lance's face, Wolf wondered if he had made a mistake in compromising. "It will be put in a safe place and not used, right, Lance?" he stressed.

Lance tore his eyes off the key. "Right. Safe. Sure, Wolf," he answered, turning on the full force of his charming smile.

Unmoved by the display, Wolf turned to Kimberly as the more serious of the two older Brentwoods. She gave Wolf a conspirator's wink and told him in a low voice, "I'll make sure it's safe, Wolf. Don't worry."

Not wanting to push the key issue any more, Peter once again asked about Catie.

"Well, she seemed really eager to work with you on finishing this quest. Some of the treasures you discovered in the crates should go to her," Wolf reasoned. "We'll have to see the level of her future interest—whether or not she would fit the role as a guardian. Her parents were content with what they found and Kimberly's father and I saw no need to involve them any further. Let's just see how it goes with Catie. All right?"

Glad to hear his friend was going to have at

least a part of this exciting future, Peter eagerly agreed. "Can I go up and see the War Room now?" was his next question.

At the expressions on the three faces that turned to him, he could see the answer was no. Unperturbed, he asked hopefully, "Some day?"

"Yes, some day," Kimberly gave him a hug. "We're really proud of you, Peter. Both for the way you worked through the quest and for the way you took care of Catie."

"She's my friend. I couldn't let her get hurt."

"Speaking of hurt, Wolf, what about Todd Raven?"

Wolf glared at Lance and wondered why he brought that up in front of the boy.

Lance understood the frown he was getting from the security guard. "He is involved in this as much as we are and deserves to know," he pointed out.

"Know how much?" Wolf asked back at him.

"Enough," as Lance's cryptic reply.

"All right," Wolf began slowly, turning to face Peter, "I am going to take Raven somewhere where he won't hurt anyone any more. He proved over and over again to be dangerous and he can't be trusted."

"I hope he goes to prison!" Peter spat out. "I'd like to see him rot there."

"Peter!" his mother exclaimed, shocked to hear such angry words out of her oldest son.

"Well," he claimed, not backing down, "he held us at knife point—twice for me—and he threatened Catie! I think that's kidnapping and something with a deadly weapon.... I can't re-

member the word.... Then there was the black-
mail thing with that other security guy. And he
stole my Gold Pass! He needs to rot in prison!"

Wolf gave an uncharacteristic sigh.
"There's more to it than just that, Peter. He's
seen too much. He's seen the War Room. He
also stole some delicate documents written by
Walt from the filing cabinets that I need to get
back. He won't forget what he saw."

"You can scare him into not talking," offered
Peter, highly aware of Wolf's intimidation factor.

"Do you really think he won't say anything if
he went to prison? Or that he won't come back
here to the house and try to get more if he got
out on bail or got released for some reason?"

"I'd like to see him try!" Peter claimed, trying
to look bigger than his thirteen years allowed, his
hands forming into fists.

"Would you want to see Andrew or Michael
or your mother put in danger again?" was his
dad's quiet question.

The words hit Peter hard. Seeing his dad's
point, he snapped his mouth shut, shaking his
head no.

"I think you can see why the authorities
won't be notified."

His eyes went wide as Peter thought of
something else. "You aren't going to...you
won't...," he broke off, not wanting to voice it.

"No, Peter, he isn't going to die. I'm just
going to take him somewhere so he can't cause
any more trouble for anyone here."

"I want to go with you," Peter declared to
Wolf. At the obvious negative reaction his state-

ment was about to unleash, he held up a hand to stop them. "Wait a second. I know you don't want me near him again, but it's my right! He held *me* at knifepoint. He threatened *my* family and *my* friends. I deserve to see wherever it is that Wolf is taking him." His mouth set in a firm line, he steadily looked at each adult in the room as if daring them to argue his point.

"I agree." Wolf broke the silence that followed Peter's outburst.

Expecting his parents to immediately oppose, Peter was amazed to see them silently considering it. He wisely kept silent and let them work it out. He had already had his say.

With a brief nod, a white-faced Kimberly gave her husband the go-ahead. "Fine, but I am going with you," Lance addressed himself to Wolf. "He shouldn't see that alone."

Accepting Lance's stipulation, Wolf glanced out the window. "The Park closes at ten tonight. Be at the dock at eleven. Kimberly? You'll call to shut down the River?"

She nodded. "I'll shut it down until one in the morning. That should give you enough time."

Peter had no idea what they were talking about. Why were they even discussing Disneyland? Todd was probably still unconscious in that hidden room, but wouldn't they just put him into Wolf's car? What dock did he mean? "River? What river?"

"Frontierland River," Wolf briefly answered from the door as he headed out. Within moments they heard the front door close and he was gone.

"What? Are we going to get a private show-ing of *Fantasmic!* or something? I don't under-stand."

Kimberly put a hand on his shoulder as she was getting ready to go upstairs to the War Room. "That's all you're going to be told right now. You'll see the rest at eleven."

"You aren't going?"

His mother shook her head. "No, Michael and Andrew are far too young. I don't want them there. I don't want you there, either," she admit-ted, placing a warm hand on his cheek, "but you probably are right. You need to see what is going to happen."

Knowing he wasn't going to get any more answers, Peter just watched as she walked up the stairs.

There were four people at the Frontierland River late that night. Father and son, so alike, were standing close together at the edge of the silent canoe dock. The large canoes used by the guests during the day were securely roped to the wooden dock. A small utility canoe that was usually stored at the far end of the Hungry Bear Restaurant was bobbing next to them in the greenish water of the Frontierland River. In the canoe, lying unconscious on his side was the ex-security guard Todd Raven. Holding a paddle and sitting on the back seat was Wolf. He had cast off his uniform's shirt, hat and shoes, set-ting them on the edge of the dock as if he hadn't wanted them to get wet. Illuminated by the bright moonlight, there was an odd white patch of hair glowing in the dark mat that covered his broad chest.

Peter silently watched as Wolf tilted his head back and let out a loud, lingering wolf howl. The sound echoed over the water and then faded out as it drifted over the tall pine trees of the Island. It was so eerily life-like that the hairs on his arms stood straight up and his heart began pounding in his chest. Peter could only stand silent and watch as Wolf pushed away from the canoe dock and slowly paddled out to the middle of the river. His eyes fixed on the far bend, his powerful arms seemed to be conserving their strength as his strokes were shallow, almost ineffective.

Breaking out of his trance-like state, Peter was about to call out and ask Wolf where he was taking Todd when a sudden wind pushed unexpected rain drops into his face. Looking past the barely-moving canoe, he could see a thick fog inching its way over the river, thin fingers of gray moving this way and that above the water.

His dad grabbed his arm when a freak bolt of lightning came out of the fog and hit the river sending up a geyser of water. About to yell a warning to Wolf, Peter saw their friend dig deeper with the paddle and head straight for the fog. "What's he doing, Dad? He has to turn back!"

"Just watch," Lance told him louder over the force of the wind blowing steadily down the river, tightening his grip on his son and backing him away from the edge of the dock.

Another lightning strike hit the water directly in front of the canoe, sending up a pink geyser of lights that swirled around and around. Seemingly unperturbed by the violence going on around him, Wolf angled the canoe to hit the lights dead center and, inexplicably, paddled even faster.

"Wolf!" Peter cried out as the tip of the canoe hit the edge of the swirling vortex and started to turn in the tide.

"He's all right." Lance tried to tell him as they took another step backwards, but his words were blown away in the violent wind.

His eyes wide, Peter drew in a sharp breath as a realization hit him. "I've seen this before. I was about six years old," as he turned to face Lance, repeating, "I saw this before! He...he said he was going home!"

His dad could only nod his head when there was another explosion on the river.

With a sudden jerk, Peter wretched his arm away from his father's grasp and ran toward the end of the dock.

Caught off-guard by the suddenness of his action, Lance was frozen in place as he watched Peter dive out into the water. Eyes wide with terror, Lance saw one last bolt of lightning churn the angry water and he jumped in after his son.

But he was too late. The river in front of him was empty. Todd, Peter and the wolf had already disappeared from view.

—THE END—

COMING IN 2013

HIDDEN MICKEY ADVENTURES 2

Watch for the exciting sequel of
Hidden Mickey Adventures 1:
Peter and the Wolf

Catie and her twin brother Alex
will embark on a new
Hidden Mickey quest
as another riddle is revealed
and they find themselves
involved in more mystery
and adventure.

Always watchful, Wolf will be
on hand guarding secrets
of the master of it all:
Walt Disney
as the legacy continues!

ENJOY ALL OF THE BOOKS BY Double R Books

IN PAPERBACK AND EBOOK FORMATS

THE GAME & QUEST BOOKS
FOR DISNEYLAND AND WALT DISNEY WORLD

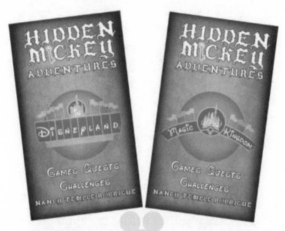

HIDDEN MICKEY ADVENTURES
GAMES QUESTS CHALLENGES
in Disneyland and WDW Magic Kingdom

ADD TO YOUR FUN AT THE PARK!
WORK ALONE, WITH FAMILY, OR FORM GROUPS
CHALLENGE EACH OTHER TO SEE WHO DOES THE BEST!

COMMENTS FROM OUR READERS:

THIS BOOK WILL GIVE YOU A WHOLE NEW WORLD OF FUN TO ENJOY!

EXPLORE THE PARK IN A NEW WAY!

PLAYING THE QUESTS GAVE OUR VACATION A SECOND WIND OF ENERGY!

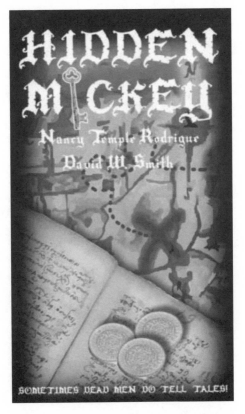

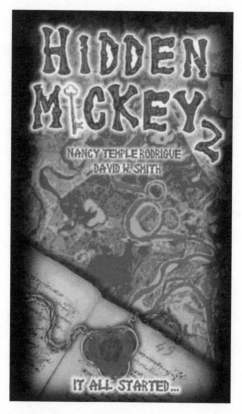

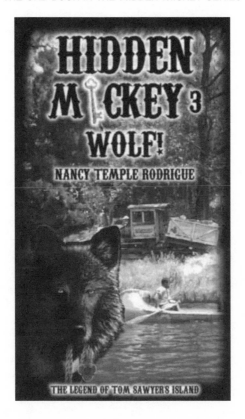